MISSION UNOFFICIAL

Lieutenant Arthur Fancy had just one question for Andy Sipowicz about the killing of Lou Nardi, the mob's button man who had been ready to turn witness for the prosecution.

"Where the hell were you?" Fancy wanted to know.

"In the bar," Sipowicz told him. "Think I'm proud of it?"

"Give me one reason why I shouldn't put you on suspension," the lieutenant asked.

"I'll give you two," said Sipowicz. "I'm gonna nail Giardella's ass to the wall over this."

"What's the second reason?"

"That I'm gonna do it with or without a badge," Sipowicz promised him. "Got a problem with any of that, Lieutenant?"

"Officially, yes," Fancy said. "Unofficially—none whatsoever."

**The NYPD has a lot of rules—
ready to be broken. . . .**

BLUE BEGINNING

NYPD BLUE

BLUE BEGINNING

a novel by
Max Allan Collins

Based on the television series
created by David Milch & Steven Bochco

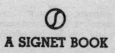

A SIGNET BOOK

SIGNET
Published by the Penguin Group
Penguin Books USA Inc., 375 Hudson Street,
New York, New York 10014, U.S.A.
Penguin Books Ltd, 27 Wrights Lane,
London W8 5TZ, England
Penguin Books Australia Ltd, Ringwood,
Victoria, Australia
Penguin Books Canada Ltd, 10 Alcorn Avenue,
Toronto, Ontario, Canada M4V 3B2
Penguin Books (N.Z.) Ltd, 182-190 Wairau Road,
Auckland 10, New Zealand

Penguin Books Ltd, Registered Offices:
Harmondsworth, Middlesex, England

First published by Signet, an imprint of Dutton Signet,
a division of Penguin Books USA Inc.

First Printing, September, 1995
10 9 8 7 6 5 4 3 2 1

For Phil Dingeldein—
who holds the camera steady

AUTHOR'S NOTE

This book is not a "novelization" of episodes of *NYPD Blue,* but an original prequel to that award-winning series.

The pilot episode presented Detectives John Kelly and Andy Sipowicz in midstream, their characters well developed, the conflicts in their personal and professional lives ongoing. When I was approached to write the first *NYPD Blue* novel, it occurred to me that it might be interesting to create, essentially, the episode *before* the first episode, to explore the beginnings of those characterizations and the roots of their conflicts.

Thank you to Bob Randisi, Tom Summit, Nancy Guy, Ralph Napolenoni, and the Palmers, Bill and Karen, for answering research questions.

My thanks to Steven Bocho and David Milch for their interest in this project, and to the staff at Steven Bocho Productions (with a special nod to Moira Kirland for the background support above and beyond the call of duty). A special thank you to editor Peter Borland at Signet Books, for giving me this opportunity.

—M.A.C.

"As a citizen, you owe it to yourself
to know something about the police,
their limitations as well as their triumphs."

—JACK WEBB

ONE

John Kelly liked to think working as a detective out of Manhattan's 15th Precinct hadn't drained him of every ounce of his humanity. But babysitting an asshole like Lou "The Lover" Nardi taxed the hell out of *that* notion.

Kelly and his partner, Andy Sipowicz, had spent the last four days holed up in this shabby two-room "suite" at the Hotel Savory in midtown Manhattan, keeping grand jury witness Nardi on ice.

The only saving grace was they were working three to eleven p.m.; Kelly didn't know if Sipowicz could stomach the indignity of the night-relief boys who had to take the daybed and a rollaway while a low-life mob guy like Nardi got the bedroom.

Nardi was fifty-something, liked to brag he looked thirty; he *looked* fifty-something, but a greasy well-groomed fifty-something—craggy handsome face, slicked-back black hair (Grecian Formula), a big man, bigger than either Kelly or Sipowicz.

Not that bony, redheaded Kelly or stocky, swarthy Sipowicz were intimidated by the man's size, or even his reputation.

Big guys only made Andy more combative. Kelly knew the older cop well—Andy had broken him in on the job—yet Kelly still had no idea why Sipowicz carried so much rage behind that blank, round, skimpy-mustached mask.

The hardest thing about this duty, so far, was keeping Andy from reaching down this bastard's throat and pulling out his various organs one by one.

Kelly would never admit it, but one thing about Nardi did intimidate him: the man's eyes. In the midst of that lumpy, pock-marked puss were the ice-blue eyes that, Kelly supposed, made the man irresistible to the ladies. That was part of Nardi's reputation, of course, and the reason for The Lover tag. Most mob guys had respectable "real" lives—wives, families, churches, charities, with the occasional mistress discreetly on the side.

Nardi had never married and was frequently seen in the company of beautiful women—actresses, exotic dancers, men's magazine models, higher-class hookers. Word was the blue-eyed slick-haired wonder had laid more pipe than all the plumbers in Brooklyn. Word was he got more ass than Sinatra.

Word also was that, before he became a power in the Marino mob, rising to the lofty pinnacle of Alfonse Giardella's top lieutenant, Nardi had been the most cold-blooded button guy around. That, in addition to leaving behind a trail of sleepy-eyed, satisfied, bowlegged female customers, he'd strewn bullet-riddled and/or throat-slashed corpses from here to Vegas.

That was why Kelly found the ice-blue eyes intimidating: not the blue part, but the ice, the coldness they promised. A son of a bitch with eyes like that could kill you without blinking.

Nardi was sitting in an easy chair, icy baby blues fixed on the tube, watching "Wheel of Fortune," guessing the puzzles but never getting them right even when they all but bit him in the ass.

"Saturday Night River!" Nardi shouted.

"*Jeez*-us!" Andy blurted. Pacing and smoking, he had his coat off, tie hanging loose, the underarms of his white short-sleeved shirt looped with sweat stains. "*Saturday Night FEVER*, you dipshit."

Nardi frowned at the set, and watched as Sipowicz's brilliant solution to the puzzle was proved correct.

Kelly lifted an eyebrow. "What can I say," he said to his partner. "You're a detective."

"I'm a friggin' genius," Andy said, scowling, blinking. His forehead was beaded with sweat.

Which was not an unusual state of affairs for Sipowicz—the balding detective was perhaps the sweatiest cop in a department riddled with sweaty cops—but the suite was almost chilly. Outside it was a ball-busting August heat wave, but in this room a window air conditioner the size of a Volkswagen

Beetle was chugging itself silly, turning the joint into an icebox.

Kelly knew why Sipowicz was sweating.

Andy needed a drink.

Nardi pointed the remote control at the TV set and clicked it off. The dapper one-time button guy, known for his immaculate, expensive, Gotti-like fashion sense, was wearing jeans and Reeboks and a T-shirt that said: "YOU DON'T KNOW ME—FEDERAL WITNESS PROTECTION PROGRAM." A girlfriend Nardi claimed he was going to marry and take with him in his "new life" had given the shirt to him as a gag gift.

"If you're such a friggin' genius," Nardi said, leaning back in his easy chair, cracking his knuckles, "why ain't you rich?"

" 'Cause the only way cops can get rich," Andy said, pausing in his pacing, "is to cohabitate with scumbags like you."

"Awww. You don't love me anymore."

Andy's face was a blob of expressionless putty. "I love you. I wanna marry you. I hear you got a lizard Milton Berle could envy and I wanna be a big part of that."

Nardi blew him a kiss.

"Go sit by the window," Andy said. "Maybe one of your ex-buddies will blow *you* a kiss."

Nardi shoved his hand in his crotch and said, "Blow this, dickhead."

Kelly never failed to be amazed at how fast his pudgy partner could move. There was no way in hell Kelly could have stopped it. Andy was simply across the room and upending the easy chair and Nardi was dumped out on the floor in a sprawl and that was that.

"Andy . . ." Kelly said, shaking his head.

But Andy was already backing off, blinking, patting the air with both hands. "Yeah, yeah."

"You wouldn't try that crap in front of Weisser, you gutless wonder," Nardi said, picking himself up.

Weisser was the yuppie scum D.A.'s office rep who was sharing this baby-sitting duty with the two cops. Right now the bespectacled baby-faced counselor was over at the Criminal Justice Building, seeing how swiftly (or not) the wheels were turning with the grand jury. Tomorrow might be the day Nardi testified.

On the other hand, Weisser had made the same trip every afternoon so far this week.

"You just shut the hell up," Andy advised Nardi, as the man righted the easy chair and sat back down.

Andy's eyes weren't blinking now. They were trained on Nardi like the twin barrels of a shotgun. Andy's eyes were blue, too, a dark gun-metal blue, hovering over shadowy circles, and could be every bit as frightening as the hit man's.

Nardi had not survived three decades in the murky waters of the mob by being stupid, Kelly knew. The man could recognize the coldness that was staring back at him. So Nardi settled back in the chair, took a *Penthouse* magazine off the table next to him, and started idly thumbing through.

Andy was pacing. Blinking again. Mopping sweat off his brow.

It pained Kelly to see his partner hurting like this. Andy needed a drink. He needed a drink bad—the way Dracula needed his midnight transfusion. Kelly knew that, only too well.

"You gotta do somethin' about this," Kelly had said to Andy only last week, finding him mid-afternoon at a stool in Patrick's, a bar within spitting distance of the station house.

"Somethin' about what?" Andy said, knocking back a shot of bourbon.

"This problem you got. This . . . come on, Andy. This drinking problem."

"Problem drinking? You can't be serious. I got great hand-to-mouth coordination. Hey, Leon! One more."

The heavyset bartender in a Hawaiian shirt had brought the bottle over, reluctantly refilled the shot glass, and Andy had downed it, quickly, without joy.

"I know you got no problem drinkin', Andy. You got a problem stoppin'."

"No, I don't. Once I pass out, I taper right off."

"Andy—"

"John. I know you mean well. You think you're doin' the right thing. So did Hitler."

"Andy—"

"It's not your business. Don't get in my business."

"When you drink on duty—"

"You're not my friggin' conscience! You ever see me take a drink on the job? You see a bottle in my desk drawer? What, you see me carryin' a flask around? Sneakin' a sip when we're out on some collar? Or takin' a nip in some hallway waitin' to talk to some witness? No." With the inexplicable pride and arcane logic of the true alcoholic, Andy added: "*I* drink in *bars*."

This week, Andy was paying for that pride. If he'd had a hip flask, he wouldn't be wearing a hole in the Hotel Savory's already threadbare carpet.

Nardi stood. "I gotta use the john." He had the *Penthouse* rolled up in one hand like he was going to swat a bug.

Andy stopped pacing long enough to sneer. "What, to lay a loaf, lover boy, or whip your skippy?"

Nardi sneered back. "I don't need your permission for neither, Sip-o-whiz."

Andy smiled at the snide mispronunciation, and his eyes had stopped blinking again. "How you'd like my permission to do a Kid Twist out that window?"

Nardi's arrogant expression dissolved into nothing; the reference was not lost on him: the late Abe "Kid Twist" Reles, the legendary Murder Incorporated killer, had taken an historic and extremely fatal nosedive out a Coney Island hotel window while under similar "ironclad" police protection.

Nardi gestured with the rolled-up skin mag. "Look, I gotta take a dump, okay? That's still legal in this state, ain't it?"

Andy said, "I think you need a disposal license for that in Manhattan. Don't he need a disposal license for that, John?"

Kelly said to Nardi, "Quit talking about it and do it."

The button guy snorted, tried to gather some dignity as he went into the can. The slam of the door was like a gun shot.

Andy kept pacing. Blinking. Sweating.

"Guardin' a goddamn meatball like that," Andy muttered, "what kinda freakin' duty—"

"This is that dirty job you heard so much about," Kelly said evenly, "that somebody's gotta do."

"Somebody oughta fit that dickhead for a cement Speedo and send him for a swim in the East River."

Kelly shrugged easily. "Maybe somebody will, one of these days. In the meantime, he's gotta testify. They say he's bringin' a big package—"

Andy turned and glared at his partner. "If he was rollin' over on Marino, or that toupee-wearin' turd Giardella, that'd be different. But this . . . this . . ."

Kelly didn't like it, either. The grand jury investigation wasn't an organized crime probe per se: It was a fishing expedition into police corruption. Rumble was that it would lead to a new Knapp Commission–style probe of crooked cops in the city.

"Friggin' witchhunt," Andy was saying. "This kinda duty ain't right, not for real cops like us. Why don't they leave this garbage to the Rat Squad."

Kelly shrugged again. "I.A.D. isn't part of this. This is strictly rhythm between the D.A.'s office and the feds."

"Then let the *feds* baby-sit the friggin' jerk!"

"Look at it this way," Kelly said. "When the

D.A.'s through with him, the feds'll take him . . .
then it'll be Marino and Giardella's turn."

"I got no love for dirty cops," Andy said, shaking
his head, sweat flying, "but this kinda shit makes us
all look wrong."

"Andy, why don't you sit down, try to relax . . ."

Andy looked at his wristwatch. "When do you
think Weisser'll be back?"

"Probably around five-thirty, six. He's bringing
deli from Wolff's."

Except for sodas and chips and such, there was no
room service in the Hotel Savory.

"Welcome to the Hotel Un-friggin'-Savory," Andy
said. "No room service . . . no restaurant . . ."

No bar.

"You want to take a break?" Kelly asked, gently.

Andy's head whirled and his eyes were almost
wild; his mouth was slack. "You, uh . . . wouldn't
mind I got some fresh air?"

"I wouldn't mind. Long as you, uh . . . didn't get
too much fresh air, if you catch my drift."

Andy's mouth twitched and he rubbed his palms
together, not looking at his partner as he replied.
"Yeah, uh, I'll . . . keep the fresh air to a definite
minimum."

There was a bar two doors down. Every day of this
duty, around this time, Kelly and Sipowicz had gone
through this charade. Every day Kelly had hoped he
wouldn't have to give his friend this out. But every
day, he had.

Andy was grabbing his suitcoat. "I'll be back before five."

"That'd be wise."

They weren't supposed to leave the room without Weisser's sanction.

The door closed behind Sipowicz just as the toilet flushed, and Nardi came out, buckling his belt, the rolled-up *Penthouse* under his arm.

Nardi chuckled as he moved across the room. "Your saucehead pal takin' his afternoon booze break?"

Kelly put his feet up on the battered coffee table, crossed his arms, and said, calmly, "Shut. Up."

"What's your problem?" Nardi settled back into the easy chair. "Squeaky clean guy like you, what's the big deal if a few dirty cops get squeezed? I heard about you."

"Really."

Nardi snorted a laugh. "They say you still got your cherry. But I bet your buddy Sip-oh-whiz has took his share'a apples offa apple carts."

"Why don't you watch some more TV. Maybe you can find some cartoons."

"You know what your partner's trouble is? Besides cirrhosis of the liver, I mean. He's jealous."

Kelly smiled. "What, of you?"

Nardi grinned as he crossed his arms. "Yeah, of me. Of all the broads I nailed. Of all the dough I made. Of how I whacked more guys than you clowns could ever guess, and yet still I'm gonna wind up in a nice tract house in some suburb in Arizona or New

Fuckin' Mexico or somethin', livin' high off the federal hog."

"Sounds like heaven."

"It'll be sweet, all right. You ever see my girl-friend?"

"Can't say as I have."

Nardi picked the *Penthouse* off his lap and flipped through, then held it up and open to a blonde with enhanced breasts and a lovely, vacant, heavily made-up face.

"*That's* her?" Kelly said.

"No, this is what she looks like. Almost a dead ringer. Except Holly's got bigger tits."

Wasn't this a Hallmark moment.

"I'm so happy for you."

Nardi's grin damn near split his face. "You're jealous, too. You got a wife like this?"

"I got a wife. As to the details, that's none of your goddamn business."

Nardi held two hands up, made a face. "Sorry! Sorry. I forget, the high and mighty, oh so holy John Kelly."

"Shove it," Kelly said indifferently.

Kelly did have a wife. A blond one at that, only dark blond, named Laura, and while she had neither enhanced breasts nor a lovely, vacant face, there was certainly nothing wrong with the ones she had. But there was something wrong with the marriage.

And duty like this—taking him away every evening this week—wasn't doing anything to help an already strained situation. Laurie hated his work, hated it for the usual reasons a cop's wife hated the work: long hours, short pay, hazardous conditions.

But most of all, Kelly knew, Laurie resented that his work held first position in his life.

So goddamn hypocritical, so typical of a "modern" woman—*she* had a career, didn't she, a life away from home; she lawyered with the City Attorney's office, and she brought her work home with her, jabbering about this case and that one, something he rarely did. If anybody had a right to be resentful, it was him.

Like, if he suggested she take a leave of absence to start a family, that made him a sexist throwback with "teenage fantasies" about making the streets safe while the little woman stayed home and baked cupcakes and kiddies in her respective ovens.

What bullshit.

Lately they'd been fighting over nothing. If it wasn't for the great sex, the marriage would've been over months ago. So, here they were, a few weeks shy of their sixth anniversary. No children. Nothing to show for six years of marriage but an apartment in Queens and escalating discord.

And great sex.

"Ya know, I knew your old man," Nardi said. He was flipping through the skin mag again.

That caught Kelly's attention, but he tried not to show it.

"How old were ya," Nardi said, "when he got killed?"

"Not very," Kelly said quietly.

Is that why you're so obsessed with this awful job? he could hear Laurie saying. *Johnny, it's tragic your father died the way he did . . . but it's not your responsibility to live out somebody else's life that got cut short, even if he was your father! Your responsibility is to live out your own life! Your responsibility is to me, and maybe to the family we can have ourselves someday!*

"Never really knew him, huh?" Nardi made a mock-sympathetic click in his cheek. "Died in the line of duty, so Johnny Boy picked up the torch. That it?"

"You drop it."

Nardi began laughing.

"I missed the joke," Kelly said coldly.

"Nothin'."

Kelly took his feet off the coffee table and leaned forward. "What's the joke, Lover?"

Nardi's eyes danced. "The joke is you, Kelly, tryin' to live up to who you think your old man was."

"I think you should be quiet, now."

"Stayin' so squeaky friggin' clean. And now here you are, lookin' after a key witness in a crooked-cop inquiry. Ain't that rich."

"What's that supposed to mean?"

Nardi slammed the *Penthouse* down on the table; he leaned forward and leered at Kelly. "Point is, you been livin' like a Boy Scout, and your ol' man? He was as dirty as they come."

Kelly was on his feet and across the room so fast, the first slap wiped off Nardi's leer. The second slap, a backhand, took Nardi out of the chair and onto the floor.

Nardi touched the bloody corner of his mouth with two fingertips; he was half-smiling. "You Micks and your tempers. Can't take the truth, can you? You wanna rough me up? Explain that to Weisser, how his cooperative witness got all messed up. How's that look to the grand jury? How's that look to Internal Affairs?"

Kelly could feel the blood heating up his face; he was boiling with rage. His late father had been one of the most highly respected cops in the department's history; from all accounts, John Kelly, Sr., of the 25th Precinct, had been the stand-up guy of stand-up guys, the soul of honesty and integrity. Nardi's words were ridiculous, insane . . . but they'd seared into Kelly like a white-hot poker.

Nardi picked himself up. For a guy who'd been knocked on his ass by two cops in less than one hour, he seemed to be enjoying himself. He settled back in his chair, leaving Kelly standing awkwardly before him.

"You ever hear of Honey Wayne?" Nardi's voice was softly taunting. "She was a stripper back in the fifties. No Lily St. Cyr, but she sure had a nice shape on her."

"What the hell are you talking about?"

"Her boyfriend was Tony Marino . . . yeah, that's right, Joe Marino's uncle. They say she killed him . . . with an ice pick."

This was way before Kelly's time.

Nardi's eyebrows rose. "And you know what else they say?"

"Shut up."

"They say your old man covered it up. Threw out the evidence."

Kelly couldn't keep himself from asking, though it came out an accusation: "Why the hell would he do that?"

Nardi shrugged; he was having a blast. "Why else? He was bangin' her."

That was enough. Kelly lurched forward with both fists ready, only this time Nardi was ready, too, and up and out of the chair with his hands balled, and there was a knock at the door.

Not a knock, really, but a kick, the familiar kick that Weisser made when his hands were filled with carry-out food.

The two men, frozen with fists poised, gradually melted as the kick was repeated.

Kelly shot Nardi a look so hard that it sat the icy-eyed button guy down in his chair. He seemed to be suddenly reconsidering whether pushing Kelly—not to mention the absent Sipowicz—to the edge like this was really a good way to spend his cooped-up time.

After all, sequestered suspects *had* done Kid Twists from time to time.

Kelly, the anger still flushing his face, went to the door. But behind the anger were questions: *Was Nardi just baiting him? Or could there be something to this cockamamy story, about the police detective father he had idolized from childhood . . . ?*

Kelly looked through the peephole and saw the distorted image of suspendered, sandy-haired, Ralph Lauren—wireframe-wearing Weisser, his hands filled with carry-out from Wolff's. Fuck, this was bad for Andy, Weisser making it back before him.

But there was nothing else to do but open the door.

And then Weisser, eyes popping behind the designer wireframes, seemed to lurch forward, slamming with the force of a fullback into Kelly, the carryout food flying, cups of soda bursting like water bombs, splashing Kelly as he stumbled awkwardly backward into the hotel room, the yuppie lawyer staggering into him, pushing Kelly off-balance.

From right and left, where they'd been plastered against the hallway walls out of peephole range, came two figures in dark suits and dark ties—they might have been lawyers or maybe plainclothes cops.

They were neither.

They exploded into the hotel room, one or both of them having shoved Weisser into Kelly, and both of them clutching nine-millimeter automatics with noise suppressors. First in was a skeletal sunken-cheeked blond whose hair was so light he seemed not to have eyebrows; pouring in after him was a broad-shouldered bruiser with a bluebeard shovel jaw, pockmarks you could hide dimes in, and eyebrows so thick and black they looked like misplaced mustaches.

Kelly took all this in a millisecond, the same millisecond he used to start clawing under his coat for the .38 on his hip, but Weisser was on top of him,

taking him down, even as the blond no-eyebrows one
was firing his spacegun-like noise-suppressed nine
millimeter over their heads at something.

Someone.

Kelly didn't see Nardi stand and take the four
shots in the chest, twitching like a bad singer croon-
ing "Volare"; but the detective heard the four *thppps*
of the gun and the accompanying quartet of yelps
that were Lou "The Lover" Nardi's last comments
on this earth.

"Get off!" Kelly said, pushing a whimpering Weisser off of him, the .38 now in hand, as he clipped
the blond in the midsection, damn near point-blank,
scorching the black suitcoat.

The blond's knees buckled, his eyes emptied of
what little humanity they'd had, and he toppled
between Kelly and the bruiser, who turned toward
Kelly and fired twice, *thppp, thppp,* one hitting the
already-dead blond, the other slamming into Kelly's
chest.

Funny. It didn't hurt. It was liked being shoved.
Then he sensed a spreading wetness not unlike the
splashed sodas, only warm. . . .

Kelly couldn't grip his gun anymore. It tumbled to
the floor.

And, then, so did he.

The last thing Kelly saw and heard was Weisser,
scrambling like a puppy across the shabby carpet,
saying, "Please God, no, no, no," with the last three
words each punctuated by a bullet in the back.

TWO

Sipowicz, feeling no pain, didn't know anything was wrong till he stepped off the elevator. A few hotel guests were peeking out of doorways, some with one foot in the hall, faces painted with various shades of alarm and curiosity.

And down by the Nardi suite, a very worried-looking guy in a blazer with an ASSISTANT MANAGER badge, a Pakistani or something, was milling around like an expectant father, repeating, "Oh dear, oh dear, oh dear," like a mantra.

But it wasn't the hotel guests or the assistant manager that alerted Sipowicz; it was the smell of cordite.

He barreled down the hall so fast he almost overshot the door. Damn near stumbling, he burst into the room, then threw on the brakes before *really* stumbling . . .

. . . stumbling over the sprawled corpse of a skinny blond in a black suit with a noise-suppressed nine millimeter near his limp hand.

Sipowicz felt as if he'd been struck a hard blow in the chest; the sight of the carnage before him literally knocked the wind out of him. Not to mention his afternoon buzz. If ever a sight was sobering, this was it.

Beyond the skinny corpse was another one: Assistant District Attorney Weisser, who looked like he was swimming in his own blood, or would have if there had been any movement.

Over by his TV-viewing chair was Nardi, on his side, eyes open, mouth open, the "YOU DON'T KNOW ME—FEDERAL WITNESS PROTECTION PROGRAM" T-shirt punctuated by entry wounds.

Blood was everywhere. Spattered, splashed, dribbled. A white shirt and a suitcoat, both wet with blood, were wadded and discarded here and there on the floor, as if by an undressing teenager unconcerned with messing up his room. The scarlet-splotched shirt had been torn off.

It took perhaps a second and a half for Sipowicz to take all this in, before blurting: "Jesus Christ!"

"In here, Andy."

It wasn't the Messiah answering him, it was his partner, John Kelly, calling to him from the can.

Stepping over and around corpses, Sipowicz, feeling woozier than drink had ever made him, found his way to the open bathroom door. John was standing at the sink, his shirt off, wrapping a towel tight around his shoulder and under his arm. Blood was soaking through.

Andy's Irish partner was naturally pale, but Sipowicz had never seen him look this white.

"I already called it in," John said matter-of-factly.

"Jesus, John," Sipowicz said, and helped him bind up his wound—it was right under his collarbone near his shoulder—and walked his wobbly partner out of the rest room and back into the company of their late guests.

Sipowicz sat his partner gently down on the couch. The stench of cordite mixed with the smell of shit permeated the room; several of the corpses had crapped their pants, an appropriate-enough response to getting killed, Sipowicz figured. The air conditioner chugging away wasn't going to help. Sipowicz opened a window.

Over at the open door, the Pakistani assistant hotel manager was peeking in. Speaking over the murmuring of the gawking guests, the manager said with absurd polite efficiency, "Can I be of assistance, please?"

Sipowicz held up his shield as he walked over; the manager stepped back into the hallway as Sipowicz stood in the doorway, speaking to him. "Everything's under control. Help's on the way. Just keep everybody away."

"You have dead people in there," the manager said.

"Yeah. We may be over occupancy, at that. Put it on the bill."

And he shut the door in the man's face.

Then, watching his step, he went to the couch to sit down next to his partner. John was staring blankly at the dead men.

"This is my fault," John said.

"*Your* fault?" Sipowicz wiped his sweaty brow with a palm. "I'm the one screwed this here up. I'm the one let *you* down."

"He was needling me," John said, his usually expressive voice dulled to a monotone. "Let him get to me. I . . . I was distracted."

"Quit talkin', just rest, okay? Just rest."

Sirens called from the open window; but not necessarily those of the ambulance coming for Kelly; New York City always sang a siren song.

John turned his blank eyes onto Sipowicz. "Don't you wanna know what went down?"

"No. You just be quiet."

"Let me tell you what went down."

"No. Just shut up and relax."

"That one there, I shot him."

"Sure you did. You did good."

Sipowicz knew John was in shock; what he didn't know was how much of this blood that got splashed around was Kelly's—how much of it was blood he had lost.

On the other hand, Sipowicz had a pretty good idea how the hit had gone down. The blond skel on the floor was one of Alfonse Giardella's bodyguards, Tony Persico. Spilled blood shared the floor with spilled carry-out soda, and several bags of carry-out sandwiches were scattered around the room.

Sipowicz figured Persico—and maybe another guy—had waited for Weisser, waylaid and accompanied him to the room and rode his shirttails in, catching Kelly uncharacteristically off-guard.

John had nailed Persico, but Persico—and probably a second shooter, who got away clean—had clipped Weisser and his key witness.

While Sipowicz found Nardi's death less than tragic, the gangster's murder meant a lot of scumbags would sleep better tonight. He wondered if A.D.A. Weisser had a wife and any kids; much as Sipowicz detested lawyers, Weisser's young corpse made a sad goddamn sight.

The hotel guests on this floor would have to be canvassed about what they saw and heard, and normally Sipowicz would've gotten right on that. But right now keeping John company was more important.

"My fault," John muttered.

"You just be quiet," Sipowicz said, patting his partner's leg soothingly, as if comforting a child. "You just rest."

"My fault . . ."

But Sipowicz knew that this bloody debacle was the fault of two men, neither of them named Kelly.

He knew it even as his insides cried out for another drink. The only thing consuming him more than his need for that drink was a burning rage, which was just about evenly divided between him and the two men responsible for this.

One of those men was named Alfonse Giardella.

The other, of course, was the man Andy Sipowicz hated most in the world.

The man in the mirror.

Forty minutes later, at St. Luke's Roosevelt Hospital, Sipowicz left the Emergency waiting area to step outside and have a smoke. It wasn't even six yet—the sun was just starting to think about going down, and Sipowicz wondered if this lousy day would ever end.

For a long time he stood, leaning against a wall, chain-smoking, fidgeting, an occasional ambulance screaming in his boiling rage down to a simmer now, as he sorted through file cards in his mind.

Like Sipowicz figured, that dead skel Persico hadn't come alone—in the ambulance, on the way over, as Sipowicz sat beside his stretchered-in partner, a lucid John had described the other shooter . . . thick eyebrows, pockmarks, perpetual five o'clock shadow. Which fit half a dozen or more Giardella goons.

And these were the file cards Sipowicz mentally riffled through.

He had just centered in on what seemed to him the likeliest candidate when a blue sedan he recognized as John Kelly's pulled into the hospital parking lot. Stepping quickly from the car, her heels clicking on the cement, was Laura Kelly, her attractive heart-shaped face, framed by dark-blond hair, tight with concern.

Sipowicz stepped out from the wall and called to her. "Laurie!"

She moved quickly toward him, a striking woman in her early thirties in a beige linen suit that couldn't quite concel her shapely figure.

"He's gonna be all right," Sipowicz told her, taking both her arms.

"This is what I was always afraid of," she said, frowning, eyes wet, but there seemed some anger mixed in with the worry.

"The bullet went through clean," Sipowicz said. "Nothin' crucial got hit."

"Oh my God," she said, barely listening to him, stepping out of his grasp. "This is the hospital where his father died . . ."

Laurie, he's fine—"

"I'm going in to see him. Is he still in Emergency?"

"They were gettin' ready to wheel 'im up to a room."

He walked her over to the entry and she went in, moving ahead of him, not looking to see if Sipowicz was accompanying her.

And he wasn't. Let the husband and wife have some time together, he thought. He'd go out and have another smoke.

Which is what he was doing, leaning back up against the wall, when a tall, brooding, broad-shouldered figure in a conservative business suit emerged from the parking lot like a materializing ghost. Sipowicz hadn't seen the Loo pull in, but here he was, as inevitable as death and taxes, casting a shadow as long as the afternoon.

Walking with an even stride, deliberate yet graceful, Lt. Arthur Fancy had the physical power of an athlete and the patience of a priest.

But underneath that patience, behind the carved black mask of his face, Fancy seemed always to be repressing an explosive rage. That was the one thing Fancy and Sipowicz had in common.

"How's John?" Fancy asked. There was no emotion in his voice, nor in his eyes. Fancy was one of those very controlled individuals who always seemed vaguely embarrassed about being a human.

"He lost some blood," Sipowicz said, shrugging. "They transfused him."

Fancy's eyes widened, just a little. "Then it's bad?"

"I don't think so. Bullet went through clean." Sipowicz pointed at the place on his own body. "Nothin' vital got in the way. The doctor I talked to seemed real upbeat."

"That's good."

Fancy's stare was an unspoken accusation; Sipowicz did a Rodney Dangerfield loosening of his shirt collar and tried to push the conversation along in a positive direction.

"I made the shooter, the dead one, anyway."

"Anthony Persico," Fancy said.

"Yeah," Sipowicz said, somewhat disappointed his news wasn't news. "Giardella's front bumper. Who I.D.'d him?"

Fancy shrugged a little. "He had his driver's license on him."

Sipowicz smirked. "And wasn't that a hell of a

piece of detective work. Who did the canvassing at the hotel?"

"Kid from the Anti-Crime Unit. Martinez."

"Did our Crime Scene Unit take the call?"

Fancy shook his head no. "The One-Three sent theirs." The lieutenant shrugged again. "It's their turf."

Sipowicz responded with a flurry of words: Loo, Kelly gettin' shot makes it *our* turf. It's obviously a Giardella hit, and that means Little Italy, and that means the One-Five takes jurisdiction. Just 'cause it went down in midtown . . . "

Fancy patted the air gently. "There'll be rhythm. Don't worry. This kid, Martinez, is taking a desk with us till further notice."

Sipowicz had never heard of any Martinez in Anti-Crime. He frowned. "Is he a detective, this kid?"

"Doesn't have his shield yet. Just a plainclothes officer. But he's got a good record . . . and a good heart."

Sipowicz reserved the right to form his own opinion. "What'd he turn up at the canvass?"

Fancy got out a small notebook, opened it, then spoke without looking at it. "After the sound of gunshots, two out-of-town guests peeked out and saw a male Caucasian running down the hallway. No weapon in his hand at that point. One of the guests saw the individual bolt into the elevator."

"How good a description did they give?"

"Real good. Heavily pockmarked, dark hair, heavy

dark eyebrows, dark suit and tie. I put them with a police artist already.

"That's fine, but I already know who it is."

"Yeah?"

This time his news wouldn't be spoiled. "Sal Viana."

Fancy's thoughtful frown was barely perceptible. "I thought you weren't there."

Sipowicz flushed; avoided the lieutenant's unfaltering—and merciless—gaze. "I wasn't. But Viana used to be Giardella's *other* front bumper."

Fancy shook his head and his smile was as small as it was condescending. "Andy, Giardella uses half a dozen different goons as bodyguards."

"I know. But Persico and Viana were a team. They're cousins or something."

Fancy thought about that, then nodded. "Worth checking. By the way, Andy, where were *you*?"

Finally, Fancy had struck the inevitable blow.

Sipowicz shrugged, as if the blow had been glancing, though inside he was reeling. "You want the story I'm gonna give the Rat Squad, Lieutenant? Or is this just between us?"

Fancy put no emotion, nothing judgmental, in his tone, when he again blandly asked, "Where were you, Andy, when your partner was shot?"

Sipowicz felt his lip curl into a sneer and couldn't stop it. His brain was telling him not to be insubordinate, but his mouth was saying, "I was down the street, in a friggin' bar. Where the hell did you think I was, Lieutenant? Whackin' off at the sperm bank?"

"No." Fancy lifted an eyebrow, set it back down. "I thought you were probably drinking on duty."

"Jeez, Sherlock Holmes has got nothin' on you, Loo. You think I'm proud of myself? I been with John Kelly eight years! He's like a kid brother to me . . ."

Or a son. Andy Sipowicz had a real son—he was seventeen, living in New Jersey with his mother, Andy's ex-wife. Sipowicz and his real son hadn't spoken in months. His real son hated him. And Sipowicz couldn't blame the boy. After all, what kind of father had he been? The kind who used his kid's bicycle saddlebags to hide a bottle of booze in.

At this point in time, John Kelly was the only person on the planet Andy Sipowicz felt close to. And he had let him down, big time.

"Andy . . . maybe this could be a sort of . . . wake-up call."

Sipowicz snorted a laugh. "What, to clean up my act, Lieutenant? Climb on the wagon? Maybe if I work hard, I still got a shot at chief, ya think?"

"I think you should give me one reason why I shouldn't put you on suspension—if I.A.D. doesn't beat me to it."

Sipowicz got right in Fancy's face. "I'll give you two: I'm gonna nail that bastard Giardella's ass to the wall over this."

"What's the second reason?"

Now Sipowicz backed away physically, but he hammered on verbally: "That I'm gonna do it with or without a badge. Might be more embarrassin' to you,

me out on a wild rampage, don't ya think, Loo. I'd
keep me under your thumb, if I was you."

Fancy studied Sipowicz so long, and so hard. Andy
had to look away. He felt like crawling out of his skin.

Finally Fancy said, "You capable of stayin' within
the lines on this?"

Sipowicz swallowed. "Absolutely."

An ambulance was howling up to the Emergency
entrance. Fancy's voice was barely audible.

"You go out of policy, I'll take you off the street,
Andy. And you won't get back on, either."

"I can live with that."

"Fancy's eyes were tightened to slits. "There could
be . . . unusual pressure on this one."

Sipowicz laughed humorlessly. "What does that
mean?"

"It means the grand jury investigation that this
witness was a key factor in was concerned with
police corruption. Dirty cops, Andy. Figure it out."

Sipowicz felt his face going tomato red. "You're
sayin' I may get accused of setting John up? Of being
a *part* of this hit?"

"It's possible." Fancy shook his head; his eyelids
were heavy. "Hell, Andy—it's probable."

"What a crock of shit . . ."

"I agree. I think, no matter what your . . . failings
might be, you deserve some sort of vote of confidence
from me, on that score."

"You mean you don't think I helped try'n ice my
partner, Lieutenant? Well, thank you very much! I
needed to hear that!"

Fancy ignored the sarcasm and said, "You're welcome."

Sipowicz flushed with shame and he said, quietly, "I . . . I did need to hear that. Thanks, Lieutenant."

Fancy looked up, sighed. Looked down. "Anyway . . . I want Giardella, too. He made us look bad today.

Sipowicz blinked, and forced himself to look right into the lieutenant's gaze, saying, "He had help."

Fancy stared at Sipowicz for a long time. The hard gaze seemed to soften, ever so slightly.

"What?" Sipowicz said, irritably.

"Nothing." Fancy nodded toward the emergency room entry. "Let's go in and see how John is doing."

Dusk was finally settling in. The heat of the day was letting up; something approaching a breeze was whispering across the parking lot.

"Loo — why are you doing this?"

"Doing what?"

"Giving me this shot."

"Because, Andy," Fancy said, "once upon a time, you used to be a great cop."

And Fancy headed inside, with Sipowicz, head hanging, following.

THREE

John Kelly had the half of the hospital room closest to the door. Hadn't seen his roommate yet, though a periodic hacking cough behind the pale blue drawn curtain indicated he did have company. You didn't have to be a detective to figure that out.

His bed cranked up to a half-sitting position, Kelly felt no pain, really, and seemed surprisingly alert, considering how dazed and pain-wracked and miserable he'd felt before the I.V. went in. They must have sent some pretty good stuff in through that tube connected to the hanging bag feeding the vein on the back of his left hand. The bag itself was on a portable stand, meaning he could skip the bedpan stage entirely and wheel himself to the john.

Funny what seemed like good news to a hospital patient.

The doctor, an East Indian named Jabbari, had a ready smile and more good news.

"We keep you tonight and tomorrow," Dr. Jabbari said, "and if everything looks good, we send you home to stay awhile."

"How long would you recommend, Doc?"

"You have accrued sick leave?"

"Plenty. I never missed a day before."

"Really? Not even the flu, Detective?"

"Not even the blue flu."

And the truth was, Kelly was so devoted to his job—no, that was the wrong word, more like *attached* to his job—he'd rather go in with a cold and fever than sit at home in bed.

"Well," the doctor said, "you should take a week. We'll need to keep track of that wound. The nurse will arrange with you to come in as an out-patient."

"That's fine, Doc."

Alone, except for the hacking cougher behind the curtain, Kelly considered the fact that (a) he'd been shot, and (b) he was in the same hospital where his father had died. He felt surprisingly okay with that. Especially considering that whenever he'd driven by Roosevelt, or worse yet called on a patient here, he'd feel a twinge of something that might have been dread, or even fear.

But now that he was a patient here himself, he felt an odd sort of relief—it was like he'd gotten something out of the way.

Foolish, irrational, but there it was: He had the sense that, unlike his father, he'd survived his gunshot wound. And there was, perhaps, some small piece of logic at work in his thinking. Even in a city as violent as New York, cops rarely drew their weapons, even more rarely got into shooting situations. You could easily go through a career without firing a round anywhere but the qualifying range.

Now he had a sense that the odds were on his side.

"Johnny?"

And there she was. Laura. His beautiful wife. Poised in the doorway, a vision in a crisp creamy business suit, the soft curves of the woman underneath that yuppie uniform a promise whispering to him as she crossed the room, her smile lovely and tragic.

He wondered how long it would take her to tear him a new asshole over this.

But then she was hovering over him, an angel of concern, arcs of dark-blond hair framing her sweet face as she stroked his cheek, then kissed him, gently, on the mouth.

"Does it hurt?" she asked, still hovering, stroking his forehead now, like a mom checking a child for fever.

"Naw. They got so much joy juice pumped through me, I feel like dancin'."

That made her smile, or at least she pretended it did.

She ran fingers through his hair. "You want to talk about it."

The heady, airy, floral scent of her perfume—

White Linen—was as soothing as her touch, and summoned intimate memories.

"Not much to talk about," he managed. "Couple Giardella thugs bulled their way in, where we were sitting on that witness, and shot up the place." He shook his head. "Killed that poor kid, that A.D.A., Weisser."

"God. How did Andy make out?"

Kelly swallowed. "Uh, Andy wasn't there."

Her eyes frowned. "Well, where *was* he?"

Kelly lifted his eyebrows in a shrug; using his shoulders for that process would be out of the question for a while. "He stepped out for a second."

Laurie smirked. "Gee. Let me take a wild guess why."

"You don't have to beat him up over it. Take my word, he's gonna beat himself up worse than anybody else could."

"Yeah." She found a chair and pulled it over by the bedside. God, he loved the smell of her perfume. "He'll drink himself into a stupor over it."

"How do we know it would've gone down any different, any better, if Andy'd been around? Maybe he'd be dead now."

She arched an eyebrow. "With a partner like Andy, that could easily be *your* future. Johnny, if you won't listen to reason—"

"You mean if I won't leave the department."

She looked mildly hurt, even indignant. "Have I ever asked you to leave?"

"Not directly."

She leaned forward, gently held his right hand. "Look. You're a talented guy. Bright. You've made a few enemies, sure, but you're respected. You're John Kelly's son. That could be valuable with the Old Boys' Network, you know."

Kelly smiled.

Laurie frowned. "What's so funny?"

"Nothing." He was thinking about Andy's name for the p.d. brass: the Chowder Society Turds.

She was stroking his hand gently, but there was a hard edge in her voice as she said, "If you insist on making the police department your career, Johnny, why not make it a *real* career? There are jobs in the department that could pay you a real salary, and you wouldn't have to get shot at doing them."

He looked at her, hard. "I didn't get into police work to play political games, or take ass duty downtown, making life miserable for real cops."

She patted his hand, let go of it, and sat looking at him with a forced smile. "This isn't a good time for this discussion, is it?"

"It's all right. Let's just not have this discussion too often, 'kay?"

She was staying with the forced smile. "If you won't consider taking the tack I suggest, would you consider something else?"

"What, Laurie?"

"Ask Lt. Fancy for a new partner."

"Laurie . . ."

She shook her head, the arcs of her hair slicing the air like pretty scythes. "I love Andy, too. He's got a great heart. But for a long time he's been a disaster waiting to happen. Well, today that disaster finally happened, didn't it?"

"I don't blame Andy for this."

"Johnny, you were lucky enough to survive it, don't—"

"Funny."

She cocked her head. "What is?"

"Before you came in, I was just thinking that. Thinking that I did something my dad didn't."

"What do you mean?"

"This is the place, you know. The hospital. Where Dad . . ."

She nodded. "I know, Johnny."

"I was eleven years old. But I can see him just like it was this morning. Lyin' here in this hospital bed, it . . . brings so many things back."

"What things, Johnny?"

"He worked a lot of long hours, a lot of late hours, Dad did."

"Really?" There was a gentle sarcasm in her voice; if anybody knew about cops working long, late hours, it was Laurie.

Kelly's smile was gentle, too. "Really. Anyway, he'd come in at night. He's sit next to my bed—like you're sitting next to me, now. Sometimes he'd say things. Sometimes he wouldn't. He'd just sit and look at me. I'd slit my eyes, like kids do, and peek at him while he thought I was sleeping. Or anyway, I think he thought that. Sometimes . . . sometimes he said, 'I love you, son.' It's the only times he said that, Laurie, but God I treasure that memory."

Laurie was standing again, hovering again, and she brushed the tears away from Kelly's cheek. "I wish I'd known him."

"Me, too."

Should he tell her? Should he tell her what Nardi said? Those lies about John Kelly, Sr.? Ridiculous bullshit! John Kelly, a bent cop? No way, no way in hell . . .

"Johnny?"

"Huh?"

"You were just staring for a second there."

"Sorry, baby."

She was wincing with concern, and curiosity. "What were you thinking about?"

"Nothing."

"You can talk about it."

Could she *know* about what Nardi said? Had he passed out and babbled? Was he sicker than he thought . . . ?

But then she said, "It's not . . . not every day that you . . . kill a man. Is it, Johnny?"

She was right, but the sad fact was, he hadn't even thought about it. The combination of shock, joy juice, and Nardi's accusations about his old man had completely removed from John Kelly's consciousness the bitter and not insignificant fact that this afternoon, he had killed somebody.

Somebody with a mother and a father, somebody with a wife, possibly, and who knew, maybe kids . . .

So why wasn't the guilt flowing through him? Or was there simply too much Demerol in his bloodstream to make room?

Right now the man John Kelly had killed was nothing more to him than a vicious animal. Maybe later it would strike him different; but not now. The dead man and his partner had killed Nardi, no great loss to western civilization admittedly, and from a certain point of view, Nardi, a betrayer, deserved what he got.

Only there was no excuse for the thoughtless brutality of cutting down that assistant district attorney, Weisser, a decent enough guy, a public servant with one of those safe jobs Laurie would prefer John have.

No, John Kelly would ask God for forgiveness for taking the life of that blond son of a bitch, and he might even light a candle for the bastard. But he didn't figure on losing much sleep over it.

"Do you know how long you'll be here?" Laurie was asking him.

"Tonight, tomorrow. Then I'm takin' a week of sick leave."

She smiled a little. "That's not like you. I'm surprised our next argument isn't about making you stay home from work tomorrow.

He grinned at her. "Hey, I don't need to be hit over the head, you know."

Her smile turned wry. "No. Just shot in the chest."

Should he tell her?

"Laurie . . . this guy Nardi . . . "

"The witness that was shot?"

"Yeah. Him. Right before this went down, he was
. . . saying things."

Another thoughtful wince. "What sort of things?"

He shrugged with his eyebrows again. "Crazy
things. Things . . . things about my dad."

She blinked. "Your dad?"

"Yeah, I know. What would a Mafia mutt like that
know about my father, anyway? It's absurd."

"What did he say, Johnny?"

"Nothin'. We'll talk about it later, 'kay?"

But she pressed him. "What did he say?"

"He . . . he said my dad was bent."

"*Your* father? That's absurd."

"Something about a murder he helped cover up."

Her smile was incredulous. "Oh, Johnny, please!
John Kelly, Sr.? He's the patron saint of honest cops
in this town. Why are you even giving this two
seconds of thought?"

He nodded. "You're right."

"What was the guy doing, giving you a bad time?
Trying to get you going?"

"Yeah, actually, he was."

"A murder." But she was interested in spite of it
all. "What sort of murder?"

"Some stripper iced Marino's uncle."

"I never heard of that. Must be before my time."

"Before all of our time. Forget I mentioned it."

"A *stripper*? And your father covered it up? Why?"

"Nardi said my dad was havin' an affair with the woman."

Now she was frowning with more than her eyes. "Oh my God. You're not—"

"Not what?"

"That's why you're agreeing to take sick leave for a week! You're going to look into it, aren't you?"

"Don't be silly."

Her expression was firm; so were her words. "Don't you be silly, Johnny. This is just some nonsense that sick lowlife was spinning, to . . . what is it you're always saying? 'Squeeze your shoes'?' "

"You're right." He twitched her a little smile. "You're right . . . but I'm still takin' the week off."

Her gaze was skeptical. "Strictly rest and recuperation?"

"Absolutely. Laurie. Do me a favor."

She teased him with a smile, and a hand on his midsection. "I don't think you're up to it, yet."

He laughed. "We got a week to work *that* out, don't we? Listen—don't say anything to Andy. Don't get on his case, 'kay?"

She withdrew her hand. "My husband's partner almost gets him killed, and—"

"Just don't. Andy and me, we'll work it out."

Now her gaze was hard. "I hope by working it out, you mean you'll ask Lt. Fancy for a new partner."

"I'm asking you to respect my business."

"Or are you asking me to mind my own business?"

"I'm asking you to respect mine. You up for that?"

She swallowed. Then she nodded. "Okay. Okay, Johnny."

"Thank you, Laurie." And he reached out and took her hand and squeezed it; she squeezed back.

"You want me to hang around?" she asked.

"Naw. Come by tomorrow, after work. Maybe they'll spring me."

"Okay. See you then."

"See you then."

She leaned in and gave him a quick kiss; he sat up and they had another, longer one. Her perfume made him dizzy.

Then she went to the door and lingered there a second, flashing him a wicked little smile. "I'll see you at home."

As she went out, she almost bumped into Sipowicz, standing out there, waiting for his turn.

"Andy," she acknowledged.

"Laurie," he said, nodding.

Andy stepped into the hospital room, closing the door behind him. "So, does it only hurt when you laugh?"

"Not even then. I'm ridin' a Demerol wave."

Andy came over to the bedside, twitching a smile, nodded at the hanging bag of liquid on its wheeled stand. "I oughta get myself one of them with a bottle of bourbon on it."

"It'd save you some time," Kelly allowed.

Andy seemed to realize how stupid his remark was, in light of what happened this afternoon. His eyes darting everywhere but never landing on Kelly, he said, "Bad joke. Listen, uh . . . Fancy's out there. Wants a word with you."

"Sure. Send him in."

The twitchy smile turned embarrassed. "I wanted a word with ya, first. Before Lieutenant Robohump gets you."

Kelly grunted a laugh at this reference to their seemingly emotionless boss. "What's up?"

"I need to ask you somethin'."

"Sure."

Andy swallowed, eyes traveling, never arriving. "We both know how bad I screwed up today."

"Coulda happened to anybody."

"Naw. I crashed, and you burned—"

"Andy, I don't want you beating yourself up over this. We got no way to know how it mighta gone down different if you were there. Hey, maybe it woulda been worse."

"Ain't that a show of support," Andy said, laughing darkly. He pulled a chair up and sat, hunching over, his eyes searching the floor as he spoke. "I'm not gonna lie to you. I'm not the AA type. This 'drinking problem' you say I got, it's . . . I don't think it's going to go away."

"How do you know till you try?"

"Look, I gotta deal with this my own way, all right? I just want you to know, from here on out, no afternoon booze breaks, okay? I don't touch a drop till after shift."

"Like you said," Kelly said easily, "you gotta deal with it your own way."

"And, if, uh . . . after this, you think maybe you need a new partner, I want you to know, hey—no hard feelings. I understand."

"Andy . . ."

"I mean it's nothing personal. And I'd like to think we could still, you know, stay, uh . . . you know, friends."

"Always," Kelly said. He reached out and put his hand on his friend's arm. "But I like the partner I got, if it's okay with you."

Andy sighed and his mouth twitched, but it wasn't a smile. "That's the thing. I won't be *anybody's* partner after I.A.D. gets through with me, unless . . ."

Kelly nodded. "We gotta tell the same story."

"Somethin' like that."

"Why was it you went out this afternoon? I forget. Some kind of medicine, wasn't it?"

Now Andy looked right at Kelly, and his eyes came alive. "Yeah. You know the trouble I been havin' with this stomach of mine. All that carryout we been eatin'. I was outta Tums."

"That's how I remember it," Kelly said.

"God bless ya, John."

"So," Kelly said, putting a period on that sentence, "what's up with the case?"

Andy seemed suddenly more relaxed—or as relaxed as he was capable. "I think we made the other shooter. It's a Giardella bumper named Viana."

"Don't know him."

Andy grunted a laugh. "Well, you ain't made a hobby out of Giardella like I have.

"What is it with you and him, anyway?"

"I don't know. It annoys me to see him so successful in his chosen field. I popped the hump rollin' drunks in Tompkins Square, my first year on. He puts on this big lovable front but he hurts people."

"I can back you up on that one." Kelly shifted in the hospital bed. "Listen, I'm gonna be out with this for a week . . ."

Andy frowned. "Is it that bad?"

"Not really. But it's a good excuse to cash in on some of that accrued sick leave."

Now Andy's frown got edged out by a sly smile. "Well, sure, but work is to you what bourbon is to me, pal. What's really goin' on? Somethin' I should know about?"

Kelly flashed a grin. "I'm gonna get to know my wife again, if that's okay with my partner."

"Hey, I don't blame you. If my ex-wife looked like that, maybe I wouldn't drink so much." He snorted. "Another bad joke. I better get Fancy in here before they mistake him for a statue and haul him out into some park somewhere for the pigeons to decorate."

Kelly laughed. "That was a better joke."

"I got my moments," Andy said, with a little toss of his head. "Just not many, today."

Andy went to the door, pushed it half-open and said, "Lieutenant? Come on in, would you?"

Fancy entered and a small smile cracked his stone

face. He ambled over and offered his hand to Kelly, who took it, shook it, as the Loo said, "John."

"Thanks for stoppin' by, Lieutenant."

Fancy dug in his suit coat for a folded form, which he handed to Kelly. "I need you to fill out this Weapons Discharge Report."

Behind Fancy, Andy was rolling his eyes. "Some bedside manner you got there, Lieutenant."

Fancy looked over his shoulder, barely. "You still here, Andy?"

"Apparently not." Andy headed for the door. "You want me to stop by tomorrow, John?"

Kelly looked up from the form. "Naw. I'm hopin' to sneak outta here with Laurie tomorrow night."

"You need anything—dirty magazines—call me."

"Will do. Andy!"

"Yeah?"

Kelly chose his words carefully. "Don't go off half-cocked on this Giardella thing."

"Oh, I won't, John. I'll be fully freakin' cocked. Afternoon, Lieutenant."

Fancy nodded. "Afternoon, Andy."

And with Andy gone, an astounded Kelly looked hard at his blank-faced boss. "You didn't call Andy on that remark?"

Zero reaction. "What remark?"

"You know how Andy feels about Giardella. And he blames himself for what happened today."

"Who *should* he blame?"

"You gonna suspend him, Loo?"

"No."

"Then . . . am I to understand you're giving him your tacit approval of goin' off on some half-ass . . . vendetta?"

"I wouldn't put it in those terms."

"But you're letting him stay on the case."

"Yeah."

Detective Kelly searched that stone face, found no clues. "If you don't mind my asking, Lieutenant . . . why?"

"I'll answer you with a question. Why haven't you asked me to assign you to a new partner?"

Without missing a beat, Kelly said, "Because Andy Sipowicz used to be one hell of a cop."

"You think you're the only one who knows that?"

Kelly squinted at his boss. "You think he'll have any trouble with I.A.D.?"

"Yes. But you'll back him up, and I'll back him. And we both know why: the only thing keeping that man going is his work. If he loses his job, he's a dead man."

Kelly knew the Lieutenant was right.

I don't have to tell you, John, what a deep dark hole Andy's been slipping into, with this drinking. Maybe this is what he needs to get himself back together."

"You're giving him something to live for," Kelly said, "besides the inside of a bottle."

Fancy shrugged.

"Remind me to tell you sometime," Kelly said, "what a stand-up guy you are, Lieutenant."

Fancy frowned in embarrassment. "You fill out

that W.D.R. I got no doubt they'll sign off on it. If ever a shooting was righteous, that was it."

"Thanks, Lieutenant."

The lieutenant nodded at Kelly and moved to the door, where he paused. "Your doctor says he recommended you take a week of sick leave. I'm gonna make the same recommendation."

"I'm okay with that . . . but what about Andy?"

"I'm putting him with somebody, this kid from Anti-Crime—Martinez." Fancy's chest made a little heave. It was as close to laughing as he came. "You don't send out a loose cannon like Andy without a deck boy to chase him down."

Then the lieutenant was gone, and Kelly was suddenly alone. Thoughts of Andy, memories of his father, the smell of Laura's perfume, and his coughing neighbor kept him company until the nurse came in, cranked his bed down, and gave him a pill that knocked him out like a nightstick.

FOUR

The 15th Precinct took in the East Village as well as Little Italy and Chinatown. The station house, on Fifth Street between Second and Third Avenue, was an undistinguished six-story sun-reflecting graystone, too bulky for the handful of trees along the sidewalk to priovide any meaningful shade. Across the narrow way was I.S. 27, where behind the chain-link fence a dozen shirtless black kids were getting in some spirited schoolyard basket-ball before this pleasant morning burned off and became the sweltering August day it was destined to be.

Andy Sipowicz, walking down from his hole-in-the-wall apartment on East Seventh, had hoped the morning stroll would clear his head; it was a hang-over cure he'd tried many times and had never found particularly successful. The sound of some kid's skateboard on the sidewalk was like a train wreck in his head; Hasidic chatter from black-clad curly-sideburned passersby was fingernails on his mental blackboard; a jackhammer and other construction racket was the sound of the world ending inside the otherwise vacant corridor between his ears.

Hell of a way to prepare for an I.A.D. chat fest.

Nodding to officers milling outside by the row of slant-parked squads, Sipowicz pushed through the double wooden doors into the blue world beyond.

And a blue world it was: washed-out blue-green walls, bright blue woodwork and window trim, the in-between blue of uniformed officers bustling through and the blue expressions of those citizens unlucky enough to have a reason to be squatting on the dark blue catching benches. Ceiling fans stirred the already stale air from pitifully insufficient window air conditioners, and already Sipowicz was removing his sky-blue suit jacket, stripping down to his short-sleeve blue plaid shirt and blue striped tie.

The (relatively) good-natured bulldog of a desk sergeant, sheaf of papers in hand, was heading back for his perch as Sipowicz crossed the high-ceilinged room.

"I.A.D.'s waitin' for you, Andy," the sarge said with glum sympathetic disgust.

"Hoop de do," Sipowicz said with a little toss of his head, moving toward the chain-linked stairwell.

The Detective Squad worked out of Room 202, at the top of the stairs. Today, Sipowicz was working his usual eight-to-four. He and three other detectives—Medavoy, Stillwell, and whoever this Anti-Crime kid was that was filling in for Kelly—comprised the Day Tour of the 15th Squad.

The bullpen area, where Sipowicz and Kelly's desks were butted together, was just to the left as you came in, in the shadow of the chalkboard duty roster, beyond the railing and the reception desk where a civilian employee answered the phone. Temps, lately. He hoped they'd get somebody permanent one of these days; some nice-looking broad, maybe, to brighten up the place.

Sipowicz, desiring a drink for the first time in the ninety seconds he'd been at work (a new record), lumbered to his desk and slung his suit jacket over the chair. He felt something or somebody hovering; it might have been a bird or a big insect.

It was Medavoy.

Detective Gregory Medavoy—forty-something, blond, with average, not unpleasant features mitigated by a perpetually startled expression—was a nice enough guy, once you got past his hypochondria and the fact that he was a human encyclopedia of allergies, phobias, and tics.

"I, I, I," he said.

"You what?" Sipowicz said abruptly. He hadn't even sat down yet.

"I, I.A.D. is waitin' for you," Medavoy finished.

Sipowicz felt ashamed of himself for expressing his impatience with Medavoy's stammering, but it didn't stop him from saying, "What, is that your business?"

"I'm on your side, Andy. I don't, don't blame you for what happened yesterday."

"Why? What happened yesterday?"

"You know, John, John, John getting shot."

Sipowicz heaved his chest. "What, is that the topic of the day around here? Tell ya what, Medavoy, why don't you round everybody up into discussion groups and we'll dig into it, after I.A.D. finishes hangin' my freakin' ass out to dry."

Medavoy backed away, looking hurt and, as usual, startled.

"Somebody got up on the wrong side of the bed this morning," Medavoy huffed, and went off to his own desk to work or maybe pout. Not that Sipowicz gave a flying shit.

Sipowicz sat at his desk and hunkered over it, rubbing his forehead.

"Detective?"

Only half-seeing the Hispanic kid who'd approached his desk, Sipowicz said, "Don't tell me. I.A.D.'s waitin' for me."

"I, uh, don't know anything about that."

Sipowicz looked up at the kid; he wasn't very tall—maybe five eight—but he had a good build on him, bright eyes, and a ready smile under a trim mustache. His short-sleeved shirt, cut by the strap of a shoulder rig, was apparently an unfortunate accident at a paint factory.

The kid stuck out his hand and leaned in, saying, "James Martinez, Detective. I guess we're gonna be workin' together."

The kid from Anti-Crime.

Sipowicz shook the kid's hand. "Don't pick out any towels and china, kid. It's a temporary assignment."

"No problem. Sorry to hear about your partner."

Sipowicz searched the kid's open face for sarcasm or anything of a critical nature, but came up empty.

"Thanks. You know John Kelly."

The kid shook his head no. "Only by reputation. But I like what I hear."

"He'll be out in a week." Sipowicz pointed. "Go ahead and take his desk. Just don't touch anything."

Martinez's grin was impish. "I can wear the crime-scene rubber gloves if you like."

Sipowicz smiled a little. He liked this kid already; an eager beaver but not a brown-nose. "You don't have to go that far."

Then, like a bad cut in a movie, the lieutenant was just standing there. Damn! How could a guy that size sneak up on you like that? How could he move that fast, that quiet?

"Interview One, Andy," Fancy said.

"They talk to you already, Lieutenant?"

He nodded.

"They talk to John yet?"

"I don't think so."

"Any tips for the condemned man?"

"Just do it, Andy."

Sipowicz looked away, and when he glanced back, Fancy was gone.

"What, no puff of smoke?" Sipowicz muttered.

"What makes somebody wanna do that?" Martinez asked from over behind John's desk.

Sipowicz was on his feet, getting back into his suit jacket. "Do what, kid?"

"Pop other cops for a living."

Sipowicz shrugged. "I don't know, kid. Maybe it's a necessary evil. Haven't you heard of the bad apple theory?"

"Yeah, maybe, but who'd wanna make a steady diet of bad apples?"

Interview One was the smaller of the two interrogation rooms, and did double duty as the closest thing the squad had to a lounge—coffeemaker, refrigerator, microwave where you could zap a breakfast roll or a sandwich. Of course, Sipowicz knew the only thing about to be zapped in here at the moment was him.

The two Rat Squad dicks sat opposite each other at the little table with their tape recorder and microphone ready, leaving a chair between them for Sipowicz.

They didn't stand as they introduced themselves— the young dark-haired one at right was Sgt. Martin, the white-haired distinguished-looking one at left was Lt. Brigham. Sipowicz had never seen either of them before; it was a big department.

They also didn't offer him a hand to shake. Despite their tape recorder, each had a pen in his right hand, poised to take notes at this momentous occasion.

"You understand," Martin said, "that you are entitled to have a lawyer or union delegate present?"

"Yeah," Sipowicz said.

"You understand," Martin continued, "that this interview is being recorded?"

"Yeah."

"State your name and shield number."

Andy did.

"Detective Sipowicz," Brigham said, "why did you leave your post yesterday afternoon at the Hotel Savory?"

His post? What was this, the cavalry?

"I've been experiencing stomach difficulties."

"Stomach difficulties."

"Yeah. You know, police work is very stressful. I would imagine you gentlemen are already aware of that fact, being police officers yourselves."

Brigham thumbed through a file folder before him. "You're not on record for any medical leave, or any medical care, related to such a condition—"

"It's not a 'condition.' I'm overweight. I get gas. I get heartburn. We were baby-sitting that witness, eatin' a lot of that rich deli food, carryout stuff, you know. I guess with my delicate digestive tract, I shoulda taken more care. Anyway, I went out for some medication of the over-the-counter variety."

"At what time?"

"Half past four, maybe."

"And specifically what 'over-the-counter' medication would that be?"

"I got 'em right here." Sipowicz reached in his jacket pocket and tossed the half-used roll of Tums out on the table. They rolled over toward Martin.

"Would you have a receipt for those?" Brigham asked.

"I'm not in the habit of asking for receipts for items like that. I would think that should I turn up here today with a receipt, that would be a suspicious act. In my opinion."

"Your expert opinion," Martin said dryly.

"Sipowicz risked a little smile. "My expert opinion."

"Where did you buy these?" Martin asked, holding up the half-roll of Tums.

"Little drug store down from the Savory."

"Do you think the salesclerk would recognize you?"

"It was busy in there. I was probably just a face in the crowd." Sipowicz nodded toward the Tums in Martin's hand. "You through with those? Or were you gonna bag 'em as evidence or something?"

Martin handed the half-roll back to Sipowicz, who peeled back the wrapper and popped one of the mints into his mouth, chewed it up, and swallowed.

"You suffering from stress right now, Detective?" Martin asked dryly.

"Naw. I just got a pain, is all."

The two I.A.D. men just stared at him for what seemed an eternity while the air conditioner whirred and chugged in the background.

"This must be one of them pregnant pauses you hear so much about," Sipowicz said.

"You have a reputation in the department," Brigham said, "as a heavy drinker."

Sipowicz could feel the red rising from his neck. "I don't drink on the job. Not even at lunch, not a goddamn drop." He sat up, straightening himself. "And, hey, you know, I'm no lawyer, and I'm not no union delegate, either, but I would venture to say you're delving seriously into the realm of hearsay, gentlemen."

Bringham's eyes were unblinking. "Do you deny that you're a known alcohol abuser?"

Sipowicz shifted in his chair, leaned forward, put his weight on an elbow, and looked hard at Brigham. "I'm known to put back a few, from time to time."

Brigham nodded in slow agreement.

Sipowicz continued: "But you've got my package there—you find any instances of drunk driving? Any complaints of drinking on the job? Any black marks on my record at all, pertaining to 'alcohol abuse'?"

"We ask the questions here, Detective Sipowicz," Martin said.

Brigham said, "Do you have any ties to the Marino crime family, Detective Sipowicz? Have you had any dealings with Alfonse Giardella?"

Sipowicz snorted a laugh. "Yeah, I've had 'dealings' with Alfonse Giardella. I been busting his ass since I was a rookie outta the academy, back when he was a cheap hood jackrolling drunks in the park. Check my record for *that*."

"Do you have any objection to showing us your current financial statements and records, to ascertain whether or not you've had any recent monetary windfall?"

"I can provide that. I wouldn't even insist on you gettin' the court's permission, like you really oughta have. I'm cooperative. You'll see my latest windfall is my fabulous last paycheck. Maybe we can all go to Acapulco on that, gentlemen."

Martin said, "You're not helping yourself with this attitude, Detective."

Sipowicz shifted his weight and his gaze toward the younger I.A.D. officer. "My partner got shot yesterday. I would prefer being out on the street finding the scumbag that perpetrated that outrage, rather than discussing my financial holdings with you two fine representatives of New York law enforcement's valiant effort to police itself."

Sipowicz stood.

"Is there anything else?" he asked. "Did I forget to mention I'm not and have never been a member of the Communist Party?"

"You don't want to get on our bad side, Detective," Brigham said quietly.

"And which side would that be, exactly? Maybe you could point me to your good side, although I wouldn't want to be accused of currying favor. Now do you want my badge and gun? Are you going to suspend me? Or could I get back to work now?"

Silence hung in the room like a thundercloud threatening to burst; but all that happened was Brigham clicking off the recorder and saying, "You can go."

And Sipowicz went.

"How, how did it go?" Medavoy asked.

"I charmed the friggin' pants off those guys,"
Sipowicz said.

A hand touched his arm, and Sipowicz turned to
face an urgency-dripping Martinez. "Sector car just
called in a dead body in an alley over on East Tenth."

"Is it a murder?"

Martinez raised his eyebrows, set them back
down. "Woman with her throat slashed and her
tongue cut out."

"That would be a murder," Sipowicz said.

She was casually dressed for an occasion as important
as the last day of her life: a baggy white T-shirt with
a supposedly comical saying made illegible by the
heavy blood spill from the gaping throat wound,
fashionably frayed jeans, designer running shoes.
Her long blond hair was ponytailed back and she
wore no makeup, and that made her look a little
plain—or maybe her natural attractiveness had been
dimished by the ghastly ear-to-ear gash under her
chin and the caked black bloody cavity that had once
been a mouth.

The dead-end alley was crime-scene taped off, and
the only company the woman had right now was
Sipowicz, Martinez, and a uniformed officer. The
detectives were wearing the rubber crime-scene
gloves Martinez had joked about earlier.

The Crime Scene Unit had arrived, and waited
patiently at the curb amid the neighborhood gawkers;
but first the detectives had to have their appraisal.

The first uniform on the scene had found her

purse in one of the garbage cans she lay fetally near: fifty-some dollars in cash, plus a VISA and other credit cards, a library card, and a New York State driver's license—all of which identified her as Holly Jane Peterson. She was twenty-eight years old. She lived on Bleecker Street.

And she was probably engaged to be married, because she wore a healthy-size diamond ring on the fourth finger of her left hand.

"They didn't kill her here," Sipowicz remarked looking down at the dead girl.

"Not enough blood," Martinez said, nodding.

"Plus the lividity's all wrong." Sipowicz got down on his haunches for a closer look. The young woman's flesh was white, except for the lividity bruising, and, even through the rubber glove, her body felt stone cold. Rigor had set in.

"I make her dead eight hours, anyway," Sipowicz said. "Dumped her here no later than dawn, probably."

"How do you figure that?" Martinez asked.

"In the dark," Sipowicz said, standing, "some homeless mutt seekin' shelter woulda stumbled on this, and helped themselves to those hundred-dollar shoes of hers. Not to mention that rock on her finger.

"If they dumped her after daylight, somebody could've seen it."

Sipowicz nodded. "Which means we should be canvassing the neighborhood."

Martinez nodded back. Then he shook his head gravely. "This is pretty vicious."

"You got a flair for the obvious, kid."

"What's goin' with this?" Martinez asked. He seemed both irritated and confused by the slaughter before him. "I mean, she was a nice-looking woman, before this plastic surgeon went to work. Jealous lover or somethin'? Was she raped and silenced, you think?"

"Neither. But for a girl with no tongue, she speaks volumes."

"What?"

Sipowicz laughed humorlessly. "This is an o.c. hit, plain as the nose on your face and the hole in hers. Didn't you ever see *The Godfather*? Horseheads in your bed and sleeping with the fishes. Stool pigeons get their tongues cut out, kid—even in real life."

Martinez threw his hands up. "Okay. All right. But she's not some dead fat goombah in the trunk of a car. This is a pretty girl. Was a pretty girl."

Sipowicz gestered to the corpse's pale face and its crusted black chasm of a mouth. "Look past the lack of makeup, and get past the butchery, too. What do you see?"

Martinez shrugged. "I see a nice-looking girl."

"You see a woman fine enough to make her living off her looks. Take a gander at those years of bottle-blond hair. Notice how slim she is. Those long legs. And I mean no disrespect, and maybe it's goulish to say so, but we're professionals, kid, and take it from a seasoned investigator, under that baggy shirt you're gonna find some of the nicest tits money can buy."

The kid frowned in thought. "Working girl? Escort service type of talent?"

Sipowicz shook his head, no. "I don't think so. I think we got an exotic dancer here. That's a stripper to an uncultured youth like yourself." ·

Martinez, looking down at the corpse, was nodding now. "I can buy that."

"Also, it explains why she was dumped here."

"How does it explain that?"

"Let's take a huge leap of faith and assume that the strip club she works in is owned by somebody mob-connected. They grab her outside of her place of gainful employment, as she's leaving work let's say, and they do the evil deed . . . but they don't want to leave her near this establishment that they own."

Martinez was nodding again. "Makes sense."

Sipowicz squinted down at the corpse; something at the back of his mind was nagging him. "Can you make out what that T-shirt says?"

Martinez knelt by her. "Yeah . . . sort of. Something about 'you don't know' . . . I think this word is 'protection.' "

"Jesus."

"What's wrong, Detective? You don't look so good."

Sipowicz felt like he'd been struck a blow. He leaned against the brick wall of the alley for a moment, then he bent down and looked at the T-shirt again himself, and said, "Jesus Christ."

Martinez, still down on his haunches, looked across the bloody, once-beautiful woman, his eyes wide with curiosity; he wanted to learn. "What do you see, Detective?"

"I see the late Lou 'The Lover' Nardi's equally late girlfriend," Sipowicz said.

FIVE

Despite his protestations, John Kelly stayed for a second night at Roosevelt Hospital, and Laurie called in to work so she could take the morning off to escort him to their apartment in Queens.

That first day home he hurt worse than either day in the hospital—his pain pills were evidently not as potent as the Demerol they'd been pumping in him at Roosevelt—and his whole body ached, every damn muscle.

Laurie sat on the edge of the bed; she was dressed for work in a crisp blue business suit with a slightly frilly white blouse beneath that served as a reminder of her femininity. Not that Kelly needed any reminding.

"You sure you don't want me to stay and keep you company?" she asked. "You're not the only one with accrued sick leave."

"If you're gonna play hookey," he said, managing a grin, "wait a couple of days, till I'm up for the job."

The smile she gave him back wrinkled her chin and she leaned in and kissed hm softly on the mouth.

"Medicine breath," he said, half-turning away.

"I don't mind." She got up and walked toward the doorway, glancing back to say, "I just might take you up on that day at home, later . . . we'll explore some natural remedies."

She blew him a kiss and was gone.

The next few hours he stayed in bed and slept, with the exception of potty breaks, trips to the kitchen for soda crackers and 7-Up, and a call from Andy.

"How's the loafer?" his partner's voice said from the bedside phone.

"Loafer is right. All I been doin' is sleepin' and pissin'."

"That's the life, all right. You musta done okay with I.A.D. I mean, it's the second day and I haven't felt any aftershocks or anything."

Kelly's late-morning hospital-room confab with Lt. Brigham and Sgt. Martin yesterday had been uneventful.

"Do you know why your partner stepped away from his post yesterday afternoon?" Brigham had asked.

"His stomach was bothering him. I think he went out for some Maalox or something."

"Have you ever witnessed your partner abusing alcohol?"

"Andy drinks, but not on the job."

"No problem," Kelly said. "How did it go for you?"

"Terrific," Andy said. "We really hit it off. We're thinking of takin' a studio apartment in the village, Brigham and Martin and me."

"Wouldn't that be cozy. So what's up with you, buddy? You start your Dodge City campaign against Giardella yet?"

"Hey, that hurts, John. You know I'm a by-the-book kind of cop."

"Oh, yeah. Only Mickey Spillane wrote the book."

"Do I need an attorney or my 'union delegate' for this conversation to contine?"

Kelly laughed, shifted in bed; then the laugh turned into a groan.

"You okay?" Andy asked. "You're not dyin' on me or anything, are ya?"

"Naw," Kelly said. "I just feel like I got hit by a wrecking ball, is all. I hope to be up and around tomorrow. I got a sling I gotta wear and everything."

"This sling, this is for your ass, I take it?"

Kelly laughed again. "So, spill already. What's up with the case?"

"You must not read the *Post*. You must be one of them *New York Times* intellectuals I been hearin' about."

"I haven't bothered with any of the papers. Laurie saw some of the TV coverage."

The shooting at the Hotel Savory, with its dead assistant D.A. and "slain key witness, mobster Lou 'The Lover' Nardi," was a hot tabloid topic. Laurie had been keeping close tabs on the situation, and fortunately Andy's drinking problem hadn't been picked up on by any of the media.

"You really owe it to yourself to pick up this morning's *Post*," Andy said. " 'Tongueless Topless.' " Sheer poetry; how do those guys do it?"

"What the hell are you talking about, Andy?"

"Name Holly Jane Peterson mean anything to you?"

"Not a thing."

"She was Nardi's main squeeze. The one he said he was gonna marry. You know, the bimbo that gave him the gag T-shirt about the Witness Protection Program."

Kelly had a sudden flash of the Hallmark moment where Nardi compared his fiancée to a *Penthouse* pet.

"I heard him talk about her," Kelly said, "but I'm not sure but that Nardi might not've been keeping her identity to himself, till he got relocated."

"The D.A.'s office confirmed that very thing. John, we found her in an alley off Tenth Street in a fatally dead contition—her tongue cut out and her throat slashed."

"Jesus."

"She was killed elsewhere and put out with somebody else's garbage. Seems she worked at the Centerfold Lounge over on St. Mark's Place."

"That's a Giardella joint."

"Is that right?" Andy said archly. "Do you think there could possibly be a connection between those two homicides? Or am I takin' a wild leap here?"

"You brought Giardella in yet?"

"We haven't have had a chance to converse yet. He's been outta town—was in Atlantic City when the Savory hit went down, with witnesses, his attorney tells us. So, then, hey—how could he have had anything to do with it? This Viana, we got an A.P.B. out on. Two hotel guests picked out his photo, but he's either skipped or gone way under."

"You're gonna go in the dead-girlfriend door, right?"

"Yeah. I spent a grueling afternoon yesterday talkin' to strippers at the Centerfold. You picked a great day to be out sick, my friend."

"Could you get anything out of these girls without sticking a dollar in their G-string?"

"They definitely weren't used to giving anything up for free. But my general take is, none of these girls knew Holly was still seein' Nardi."

"*Still* seein' Nardi—then they knew she and Nardi were an item at one time?"

"Oh, yeah. But when The Lover turned state's witness, Holly apparently put on a big show about what a weasely stool-pigeon bastard Nardi was. How she could never be with a man who would rat out a wonderful human being like her lovely employer, Mr. Alfonse Giardella."

"So she wasn't just a stripper, she was an actress, too."

"Well, if she'd really had her acting chops down, she might not've wound up in that alley yesterday."

"Good point. You seem to be makin' out okay without me."

"Oh, yeah. I can interrogate naked women without much help·at all. And tell ya the truth, this kid from Anti-Crime, he's okay."

"Maybe I shouldn't bother comin' back at all."

"Well, I'm glad you brought that up. I been meanin' to talk to you, John, about this burden I have, carrying you on my back like this."

Kelly laughed again, and again it turned into something more like a groan.

Andy's voiced was hushed with concern. "Hey, you need anything? You need me to drop by?"

"Just stay on the job," Kelly said. "Keep me posted, and I'll see you in a few days."

"No problem," Andy said, and hung up.

Kelly got up, took a pee and a pain pill, and returned for a nap that lasted till late afternoon. He woke from a dream about his father.

Usually when he awoke, a dream slipped away immediately, but this one—at least one image from it—stayed crystal clear, not just in the minutes that followed waking, but through the whole rest of the day. Somehow, he knew this dream, this one piece of it anyway, would stick with him for a long time.

No, not just for a long time, but for as long as he lived, cherished like every memory he had of his old man.

In the dream, it was his eleventh birthday party, and a lot of his friends were there, kids from school, some relatives, his cousins, and his two younger sisters of course; they *had* to be there. But his father wasn't, his father was working . . . and then, just as his mother was about to cut the cake, his father—in that raincoat, that trenchcoat, that so labeled him a detective—came roaring in, saying, "Hold everything! This isn't an official birthday unless *I* cut the cake."

And, sure as you're born, his father did cut the cake, and gave the first piece, a great big piece to John, smiling at him, saying, "I loved you, son."

Not *I love you*—but "loved."

In the dream, his father had then ruffled his son's hair, as he so often had in reality, and John had awakened, and then—detective that he was—he took the dream apart, examining the evidence, studying the clues.

The dream had been very much like John's real tenth birthday. His father had come home late, well into the party, but had made the little speech about the birthday not being "official" unless *he* cut the cake . . . but of course Dad had not said "I love you, son" let alone "I loved you." The only instances Kelly had ever heard his father say that were, as he'd revealed to Laurie, those times his dad had slipped into his son's room and spoken to what he'd thought was a sleeping child.

But on Kelly's eleventh birthday, his father hadn't come home late; he'd missed his son's birthday entirely. Of course, John Kelly, Sr., had had a very good excuse for missing the festivities. It had been that afternoon that Detective Kelly had gone into the wrong door . . . and never came home again.

When Kelly got up on his latest bathroom jaunt,

he knew what he had to do. Despite the throbbing pain near his shoulder, he stood on tiptoes as he probed the top shelf of the front closet, where behind winter hats, scarves, and gloves he found the hatbox. He pulled it down and carried it to the kitchen table, where he lifted the lid on the past.

When Mom's Alzheimer's got bad last summer, he and his sisters had been forced to put her in a rest home in Newburgh. Then they'd had to deal with her possessions as if she had already died; it was a heart-wrenching experience, sorting through their mother's things, putting the house up for sale, and dividing up the few pieces of furniture anyone was interested in. This hatbox contained the few personal family items he'd chosen to keep for himself.

Photos, report cards, certifications, diplomas, the usual precious refuse of a family's life. But among the paper was some steel: his father's shield. Medals of commendation. Of valor. His father had been one of the most highly decorated officers in the department's history—and he'd died a relatively young man, at forty-five.

One of the photos, taken the last year of his life, showed John Kelly, Sr., at work, at his desk at the Two-Five, grinning at the camera while a tall, prematurely white-haired detective with a hawkishly handsome face leaned in behind him, with a hand on Dad's shoulder. The detective was his dad's colleague and best friend, Frank O'Keefe.

He lingered over these artifacts, touching them,

connecting with his, and his father's, past; but none of this was what he was looking for.

The object of this search was a brown leather spiral, the newest item in the hatbox: his mother's address book. She had used it to write her Christmas cards, to keep track of friends whom time and retirement had scattered not just around the city, but the country.

Mom didn't need it now, though she frequently visited many of her friends in the time-shifting delusions that characterized her progressive mental deterioration.

Kelly thumbed through the pages, landing at "O"—and there he was: Frank O'Keefe.

His father's longtime partner in the 25th Precinct had retired some years ago to Florida—Hollywood, Florida, where there was a considerable contingent of retired cops from all around the country. Next to O'Keefe's name was that of his wife, Maureen, who had been as close to Kelly's mom as his dad had been to O'Keefe. A photo of Mom and the sparkling-eyed, redheaded Mrs. O'Keefe was in the hatbox.

Mrs. O'Keefe had had some shape on her; he had no memory of noticing that as a kid.

If Mr. and Mrs. O'Keefe weren't home, there were other names to try, other friends, colleagues of his dad's; but first he would try the man who'd been to John Kelly, Sr., what Andy Sipowicz was to him.

He took the little leather book back to bed with him, propping up several pillows, getting positioned, getting as comfortable as a man with a fairly fresh hole in his chest can make himself. Then he pushed buttoms on the nightstand phone and let it ring.

He was on the tenth ring and about to give up when the phlegm-cracking voice of a man awakened from a deep slumber said, "This is O'Keefe."

Then there was an immediate sound, if muffled, of a throat being cleared.

"Sorry," the voice said, and he repeated: "This is O'Keefe."

"John Kelly, Jr., Mr. O'Keefe. Hope I didn't disturb you."

"Johnny! What a fine surprise, hearin' your voice again."

O'Keefe had the faintest tinge of third generation brogue.

"Where are you, son?"

"I'm calling from home, from Queens."

"Why, I would have thought you were down the block."

"Yeah, it is a good connection. How have you been, Mr. O'Keefe?"

The voice, phlegm-free and strong now, came back with good-natured mock irritation. "Will you once and for all finally learn to call me Frank! How many times do I have to ask you, boy?"

"I always respected you, Frank. I'd never want to cross the line with you."

"There's no line-crossing when two men are standin' on the same side. You know, your father wasn't just the best partner I ever had. He was the best friend I ever had. The day doesn't go by that I don't think of him. That I don't miss him."

"Me, too. Me, too. I admit I feel . . . cheated, only knowing him from a kid's point of view."

"You have a right to feel that way. You wouldn't have just loved him, Johnny—you woulda liked him. You know, the reports I get from my spies up north are you've lived up to his well-deserved reputation. That would be one hell of a shadow for a son to have to stand in, in the department. My hat's off to you, Johnny."

"I appreciate that, Mr. O . . . Frank. How's Mrs. O'Keefe?"

"Maureen, rest her soul, passed on last August. Almost a year now."

"I'm sorry. I didn't know."

"No need to apologize. No way for you to know. I mean, your lovely mother, if she were herself, she would know, and she would tell you. But the dear girl . . . how is she doin', Johnny?"

"She's happy. Content. Nothing wrong with that. Sometimes she's as clear as this phone connection. Other times, she thinks Dad just went down to the neighborhood store for groceries. Sometimes . . . she thinks I'm him."

"Well, God love her, at least she has the pleasure of his company. I envy her that, and the peacefulness."

"And your boys?"

"Oh, fine, fine. Robert's in Tucson with that

computer company, and Harold's made a life in the department, you know."

"Yeah, I know, an inspector. He had quite a shadow to live up to himself. You must be proud."

"I am, but it makes me feel old, Johnny. You know, *he'll* be eligible for retirement in a couple of years."

"How are you gettin' along, Frank?"

"There's a whole retirement community down here, Johnny, and I been seein' the widow of Lt. Jack Riley of Philadelphia. A homicide man, he was. She's a young one—not seventy yet—but I'm up to the challenge."

"How old *are* ya, Frank? I admit I kinda lost track."

"I'm closin' in on eighty, and I feel just fine. The eyesight, the hearing, they're not one hundred percent; I have my aches and pains and I'm one sorry constipated son of a bitch. But like the man says, every day above ground is a good one. And what about *your* love life, Johnny boy?"

"Remember that girl Laurie I was dating?"

"Certainly do. Lovely girl, lovely child."

"Well, I married her. No kids yet . . . but we're talkin'."

"I'm happy for you, son. Love of a good woman—not a thing like it in this world."

"Frank . . . I need your help."

"Why just name it, Johnny, anything for John Kelly's—"

"That's just it. You might not want to answer some of the questions I have."

"What do you mean, son?"

"I heard something about my father the other day. Something that really bothered me. Something bad."

"Johnny, your father was a bloody saint—"

"No, he wasn't. You said it yourself: he was a man. And it's probably time I understand that, come to grips with it. It might make that . . . shadow you talked about, easier to deal with."

There was a long pause; even with a connection this good, some long-distance crackling tickled Kelly's ear as he waited for his father's partner to respond.

Finally, with some of the brogue out of it, the voice returned: "What did you hear?"

"I heard he covered up a murder."

O'Keefe's response was immediate—almost as if he knew what question was going to be asked.

"Ridiculous. Forget about it. Say, Johnny, are you still goin' to the Emerald Society?"

"Naw, I can't keep up with that kind of drinkin'."

"Did you know I used to be the best damn piper in the Emerald Society's Pipers Band—"

"Frank. This murder—it was Tony Marino. He got it with an ice pick."

"I remember. There was a shrug in O'Keefe's voice. "It was your standard mob rubout. His girlfriend came home to her penthouse and found her sugar daddy dead as Lincoln. With a sharp-object hole in him that was probably an ice-pick wound, only they never found the weapon."

"So this is an unsolved o.c. hit we're talkin' about, Frank, right?"

"Yeah, and who cares? Let those guinea goons bump each other off till Jesus comes. Who gives a rat's ass?"

"Not me, but you know, Frank, I heard it was *multiple* stab wounds. Sounds more like a crime of passion than some button guy's handiwork, to me."

"Maybe the boys were sending a message."

"Maybe. Maybe." Kelly shifted in bed; the pain helped him press on. "Tony Marino's girlfriend—her name was Honey Wayne."

"If you say so."

"Some sort of stripper or showgirl or something."

"You don't say."

"What I heard that disturbed me, that bothered me, was that she and my dad had a thing."

"Johnny, Johnny—there's nothin' down that road—"

"That this . . . relationship they had led to him covering up her murdering Tony Marino."

"There was never a whisper of that in the department. Not a whisper."

"I didn't ask you that, Frank. You were his best friend. His partner. His brother in blue. *You* know. I'm his son. *Tell* me."

"Tell you what?"

"Did he do it?"

"Johnny, this is not a line of discussion I care

to spend this valuable portion of my waning years pursuing. I got a date tonight. You mind, son?"

"Did he do it?"

"Do what?"

"Bang the stripper. Help her cover up a kill. Did. He. Do. It."

Long pause.

"I don't wanna talk about it. Nice hearin' from you. Regards to your sisters, and the little woman. Good-bye, Johnny."

And the phone clicked dead.

Kelly grimaced, hit "REDIAL," then thought better of it and slammed the phone into its cradle.

Two minutes later, give or take a second, the phone rang. Kelly picked it up. Without a beat, O'Keefe started in.

"Suppose there *was* something to any of it. Some small grain of truth. What good would it do anybody, at this late date? Your mother, God love her, you wanna tell her? Even if she had the capacity to absorb it, Johnny, what would be the point? You want to tell your sisters? What's the purpose, again? To tarnish your loving father's memory in the girls' minds? Leave it lay, Johnny, that's my sincere heartfelt advice to you, son."

"Then he did do it."

The phone clicked dead again.

Kelly spent the next half hour making calls and getting nowhere. One former colleague of his father's had passed away. Three others had answering machines taking calls—retired people were apparently busy. Two calls he let ring forever and got no answer.

Then the phone rang again.

"Johnny," O'Keefe said, and his voice was soft, all the bounce, if not all of the brogue, out of it. "It's the one thing he never told me."

"God's honest truth?"

"God's honest truth, son."

"But you suspected."

A long pause.

"I suspected," O'Keefe admitted.

"I have to know."

"I can see that."

"How do I do it? Where do I start?"

"Where else? The woman."

"Honey Wayne?"

"Honey Wayne."

"Is she alive?"

"Last I heard."

"Where?"

"I'm not sure."

"Where do I look?"

"You're John Kelly's son aren't you?"

"Hell, yes."

"Then you're a detective."

"You bet your ass I am."

"Good, then find her."

And the phone clicked one last time.

SIX

Minetta's Ristorante Italiano on Mott Street was the brick-faced street-level establishment of a typical Little Italy tenement. It was a quarter past two and the afternoon was shimmering with heat; the streetside tables of cafes and bakeries weren't doing much cappuccino business right now. Shaved Italian ice stands had the best thing going.

Sipowicz, driving, pulled a minor miracle and found a parking place on Hester, within a block of the restaurant. He would've rather won the lottery; the odds were about the same.

Martinez got out on the passenger's side of the unmarked car and said, "You know it isn't cheap, eatin' down here. This is for tourists and mob guys."

"Really," Sipowicz said, getting out. "Well this'll be my treat."

He joined the younger cop on the sidewalk. They'd

spent the morning at the Centerfold Lounge, where
the manager had reluctantly arranged for his night
dancers to come in and be interviewed there. They
didn't look as good in the morning light as they did
in evening dimness.

The interviews had gone well enough—there was
one girl out sick that Sipowicz still had to catch
up with—but cooperative though the dancers were,
nothing vaguely incriminating against Giardella had
come out of the effort.

They had worked straight through the lunch
hour—Martinez hadn't complained, hadn't even
mentioned it; Sipowicz was starting to think they
had a cop in this kid—and Sipowicz had suggested
they tool over to Little Italy for a late lunch.

Now, walking next to Sipowicz, the kid gazed at
the older man, eyes bright but confused.

"Detective," Martinez said, "is this lunch, or are
we on the job? Isn't that Giardella's restaurant, on
the corner there?"

Under his brown sports jacket, Sipowicz's yellow-
and-white striped shirt was soaked. He loosened his
black-dotted red tie, craning his neck above his collar
like a turtle restless in its shell. "You ever been on a
roller coaster, kid?"

"Sure. Lots of times." His little-kid grin was infec-
tious, though Sipowicz didn't catch it. "I used to take
my little brother out to Coney Island all the time."

"Thanks for sharing," Sipowicz said, walking
toward the restaurant. "So, you ever fall off of one?"

"Roller coaster? 'Course not."

"How'd you manage that?"

"I just keep my head up and my ass down."

"Words to live by." Sipowicz nodded back toward the car. "You wanna sit this out, no problem. Unless, of course, you *like* roller-coaster rides. . . . "

"I'm up for that," Martinez said with a shrug.

As they came in, the bar was over to the left, doing no business; a bull-neck bartender in black vest and black necktie glowered at them. Sipowicz had entered this particular lion's den before.

The joint was deep-brown paneling and a few plants and hanging caricatures and photographs of show business personalities with Italian heritage. Air conditioning made the place chilly, damn near meat-locker cold. Sun filtering in from the street windows gave the front half a golden glow, but as Sipowicz—with Martinez following—moved deeper into the recesses of the almost empty restaurant, it got darker and darker.

At the rear booth where he held court, Alfonse Giardella sat with a bodyguard on either side, one with light-blue eyes in a face that was a sea of zits, the other a pretty boy with a greasy pompadour about four decades out of style.

Giardella was a big man, wide-shouldered, corpulent, six foot-something when standing, his oval face dotted by tiny, hard, dark, close-set eyes, thick, fleshy lips indicating a beastly sensuality, with just enough double chin under his cleft to suggest a certain softness. A gold chain made its fashion statement around a neck as wide as the big head. His double-breasted suit was a dark-blue thousand-dollar number over a bargain-basement blue-and-red striped sport shirt. His hair was slightly curly, well greased, and blacker than you could find in nature; part of it was hair dye, along the back and sides, but most of it was the toupee that perched precariously on his Neanderthal forehead.

A nearly full glass of ice tea sat in front of him, as did an empty wineglass, and a half-eaten dish of pasta with red sauce had been pushed away. The gangster's hard little eyes peered over the top of a sheaf of computer printouts he was going over, as the two cops approached.

"So the computer age comes to the adult entertainment king," Sipowicz said.

Giardella dropped the printouts. His tiny eyes got even smaller as he stared up at the two plainclothes officers with contempt colder than the discarded pasta. "What do you want, Sipowicz?"

"I hear you put out a mean tortellini," Sipowicz said, with a facial shrug. "I was over at your club talkin' to the girls, and time kinda got away from me. Thought I'd head over to your fine establishment and have a little afternoon repast."

"Kitchen closes at two, Sipowicz," Giardella sneered, bobbing his head. "Come back at four . . . or were you gonna *drink* your lunch?"

"I'm not thirsty. You forget somethin', Al?"

The tiny eyes were dull and dead. "What?"

"You were supposed to check in with us, over at

the One-Five. Didn't your attorney so notify you? We got a few questions."

Giardella began looking at the printouts again, idly. "The wife and me just got back from Atlantic City this morning. I got a condo over there."

"Ain't that peachy." Sipowicz snatched the sheaf of computer printouts from Giardella's hands. Started looking them over. "So, business is pretty good in the jack-off trade, huh?"

Giardella was the Marino family's man in the blue trades—pornography, strip clubs, peep shows, adult bookstores, and the like.

"It's legal," Giardella said, grabbing back the printouts. "You got somethin' against people indulgin' their personal freedom, their constitutional rights?"

"No. I stand firmly behind the individual citizen's rights to get his rocks off."

Giardella shrugged. "Then what's your problem?"

Sipowicz leaned in so far his nose almost touched Giardella's. "My problem is my partner's constitutional right to not have some asshole shoot him in the friggin' chest."

The two bodyguards were starting to rise.

Martinez said pleasantly, "You don't have to get up on our account, guys."

The kid's hand was on the butt of the .38 holstered under his left shoulder.

Giardella waved them to sit, as he backed as far away from Sipowicz as he could, saying, "I'm sorry about your partner. But I hear he's doing okay."

"It's the principal of the thing, Al. You don't shoot cops, or even assistant D.A.'s. It's not friendly. It's uncivilized. It might even be unconstitutional."

The thick lips sputtered. "I didn't shoot nobody! I got witnesses as to my whereabouts the entire time."

Sipowicz tucked his hand gently under the lapel of Giardella's suit coat; he was still right in the mobster's face. "Nice material, Al. You come a long way from your jackrollin' days."

"This suit is two weeks of your salary, Sipowicz. Think about it."

"Maybe I should save up. You know, I'm bein' thoughtless here. I should be offerin' my condolences."

"For what?"

"Your former associate, Anthony Persico, he's recently deceased, having gotten in the way of my partner's service revolver."

"He's no longer in my employ."

"Of course not. He's a freakin' corpse. What about Salvatore Viana? Is he still in your employ?"

"Actually, no. Not for the past six months. I haven't seen Sal in I don't know how long. You see him, Detective, you give him my regards."

"Well, if you don't mind, Al, I'll just give him *my* regards."

Giardella's tiny eyes tightened; some of it was anger, but some of it was fear. Sipowicz relished that.

"Is there anything else?" Giardella said. "I'm a busy man. I got business to attend to here."

Sipowicz backed away. "This wasn't your inter-view. Your attorney wasn't present, for one thing. For another, this was just a friendly little luncheon visit. But that is a good idea."

"What is?"

Sipowicz nodded toward the front. "Goin' in and talkin' all this over, at the station house."

Giardella shook his head no. "I'll come in at my own convenience with my attorney, you don't mind."

Sipowicz glared at the fat mobster. "Oh, but I do mind, Al. I go out of my way to do a little business at your restaurant, you tell me the kitchen's closed. I invite you over to the station house for a little gab session, and you insult me like this."

Giardella grunted, tossed out his chest. "Let's see your warrant. Otherwise, I'm not goin' anywhere."

"I don't need a warrant if I witness a crime being committed with my own eyes."

"And what crime would that be?"

"Smugglin' dead muskrats without a license," Si-powicz said, and he yanked the toupee off Giardella's skull and flipped it across the room like a Frisbee.

"You bastard!"

Giardella's hands rose to his bare pate, like a surprised naked woman covering her private parts.

Both bodyguard guards scowled and started to rise, and Sipowicz dumped the pasta in the lap of the blue-eyed one, the red sauce running smearingly down his neatly pressed pants. Then Sipowicz cracked the dish over the head of the pretty-boy

bodyguard, stunning him. Not cuttng him or anything.

Martinez had his gun out.

"You whacked-out son of a bitch!" Giardella said.
He was still seated, glowering up at the detective.
"Get out of my establishment. Get out now, or I'm
bringin' charges!"

Sipowicz shrugged. "I suppose all things considered, wearin' that rug is a minor offense. I can let it
pass, this time."

The detective went over and picked up the toupee
and brought it back, dusting it off thoughtfully as he
returned to Giardella's booth, then flipping it onto
the table, into some spilled marinara.

"You're deranged, Sipowicz! Get the hell outta
my joint!"

Sipowicz held up his palms. "We're leavin' . . .
but I expect to see you and your esteemed counsel,
at the station house, by three-thirty."

Giardella laughed humorlessly. "Or what, Sipowicz?"

"Or me and my young protégé here are makin' a
new career outta going into your dens of erotic
literature and makin' sure none of your customers
have got themselves involved with indecent exposure
situations, lewd and lascivious conduct, that kinda
thing."

"Hummer busts." The hatred was radiating off
Giardella like heat off asphalt. "That's the story of
your life, you nickel stiff."

Sipowicz shrugged. "Maybe so. But citizens in this

country have a constitutional right not to have to be sickened by immoral perverted acts in public places. See you at three-thirty, Al?"

Giardella, his face damn near as red as the pasta sauce, said nothing.

To the blue-eyed bodyguard with sauce on his lap—a man, still half-standing, who was staring at Sipowicz with as much hatred as Giardella—the detective said, pointing to the smear of red on his trousers, "Little club soda'll take that right out."

Then Sipowicz swaggered out, tugging his collar with a finger, while Martinez backed out, not putting his gun away till they got back out on the street.

"Handle yourself pretty good, kid," Sipowicz said.

"Like I said," Martinez shrugged. "I been on roller coasters before."

"You wanna grab lunch over in the precinct somewhere? Then we could eat without takin' out a freakin' bank loan."

The kid grinned. "I don't think they close the kitchen over at Rokka's Coffee shop."

"Jeez, you know, you could be right," Sipowicz said, unlocking the parked car. "But do we have reservations?"

"I always got reservations about eatin' at Rokka's," Martinez said.

The 15th definitely had themselves a cop.

At 3:25 P.M., Alfonse Giardella—in the same expensive suit but now wearing a dark blue shirt with a shades-of-blue striped tie—arrived at the 15th

Precinct. At his side, steering him along like a muddled senior citizen, was James Sinclair, a fifty-something, cueball bald, hawkish-featured attorney, dapper in a dark blue suit with gray-blue patterned tie, blue-pinstriped white shirt and splash of blue pocket handkerchief, leather briefcase in hand. The desk sergeant sent the two men up to Room 202, the detective squadroom, where Sipowicz looked up from his desk with a smile.

"I'm glad you could join us, boys," Sipowicz said affably, getting up, coming over, gesturing down the hall. "I think you both know where Interview Two is."

Sinclair's smile was beyond smug. "Detective, before we go anywhere, I'll need a word with your superior."

Sipowicz shrugged elaborately. "You know, Mr. Sinclair, I like to think that no man is my superior. This is America, I like to think all men are created equal. Maybe you were out sick the day they went over that, in law school."

"Coincidentally," Sinclair said with smooth condescension, "this is just the very attitude I intend to take up with your superior."

"Well, he pretty much agrees with me on this equality issue. He's a black guy. Interview Two?"

Soon Giardella and his attorney were seated with their backs to the holding cage commonly referred to as the pen. Lt. Fancy was seated at the head of the banquet-style table, like a father at a family feast. Sipowicz was milling around the room, which was three times as large as Interview One. This interrogation chamber had a fingerprinting station at the right as you came in, smears of smudgy black making an abstract blossom around the print counter, while at the left wall was a mirror—two-way glass. Interview Two was also used for show-ups.

The indignity, the implicit insult, of being questioned in an interview room normally used for more serious, dangerous suspects, with the holding pen at their backs, was not lost upon either Giardella or his counsel.

"You understand that this is an entirely voluntary appearance," Sinclair said.

Fancy gave the lawyer the barest nod.

"I'm just tryin' to do my civic duty, here," Giardella said.

"We are willing to make a statement," Sinclair said, "as to Mr. Giardella's whereabouts during the shooting incident—"

"That won't be necessary," Fancy said. "There's never been any suggestion that your client did the actual shooting. One of the dead assailants, Anthony Persico, was in your client's employ—"

"Should it become necessary," Sinclair stated with a tiny smile, "we can provide access to the company records of Giardella Entertainment Enterprises, which will clearly demonstrate that Mr. Persico has not been in Mr. Giardella's employ for some time. Nor has Salvatore Viana, who I understand is another former employee of Mr. Giardella's that you're seeking in relation to this matter."

Fancy nodded to the briefcase in front of Sinclair on the table. "Did you bring those records with you?"

"Certainly not," Sinclair said. "But we'd be happy to provide them—should you produce a court order requiring us to do so."

Sipowicz, leaning against the table with both hands, said, "So you were in class that day, then? Court order day?"

"Lt. Fancy," Sinclair said, looking not at the lieutenant but at Sipowicz, the attorney's condescending contempt for the detective oozing out of half-lidded eyes, "are you aware of the systematic campaign of intimidation this . . . officer . . . has been venting upon my client?"

"Yeah," Giardella said, shifting his considerable weight in his chair, "he's been ventin' all over my ass."

"No," Fancy said. "But I'm aware it's taken you and your client two days to respond to our requests for this informal interview. This is a multiple murder investigation, Mr. Sinclair—and it involves an assistant district attorney as a homicide victim, not to mention the shooting of a police officer."

"*This* officer," Sinclair said, nodding toward Sipowicz, "came into my client's place of business this afternoon, and verbally and physically abused my client—"

Giardella slapped the air, gesturing toward Sipowicz. "This head case dumped marinara sauce all over my cousin Vinnie's pants!"

"I saw that movie," Sipowicz said. "*My Cousin Vinny*. It wasn't bad."

Fancy gave Sipowicz a brief but withering stare. Then the lieutenant returned his gaze to the attorney. "If this incident took place as you described, maybe you'd like to file a complaint."

"Sinclair's smile was a thin curving line. "No. We wouldn't want to cause you the trouble or the embarrassment, Lieutenant. As my client said—we're here as a matter of 'civic duty.' But perhaps you might explain to your subordinate the meaning, and the possible consequences, of such continued harassment."

"Isn't that where you keep puttin' your hand on your secretary's ass?" Sipowicz asked, mock-innocent.

Fancy said, "Could your client aid us in locating his former employee, Salvatore Viana?"

The attorney shrugged, looked toward his client. Giardella shrugged, too.

"I dunno," Giardella said. "Last I heard he lived in Brooklyn someplace."

"Thanks for narrowin' it down," Sipowicz said. "Before, all we knew was planet Earth."

Sinclair was smiling the smug smile, shaking his head; with that shining bald pate, he looked like a big, evil baby. "You see, Lieutenant? This is the attitude my client has to continually put up with."

"What's his problem, anyway?" Giardella asked, hands spread palms up. "Wha'd I ever do to him, anyway?"

Sipowicz leaned across the table, spoke through bared clenched teeth. "You got my partner shot up, you wig-wearin' douche bag."

"No! *You* got your partner shot up, you saucehead scumbag! You blame *me* for your—"

But that was all Giardella got out before Sipowicz flew across the table, sliding across on his stomach like a kid on a sled, and fixing his fingers on the mobster's fat neck; he could feel both the flesh and the gold chain beneath his grip as he dug in.

"Lieutenant!" the attorney cried out, leaping out of his seat, clanging against the wire mesh of the pen behind him.

Fancy didn't rise. He merely issued a bored little sigh and said, "Detective. Please."

And Sipowicz, face red, released his grip, but his face was once again in Giardella's. The detective whispered, "Your fat ass is mine."

"In your dreams," Giardella said, but he was shaken.

With as much dignity as he could muster, Sipowicz pushed himself back off the table, using both hands to straighten his suit jacket.

"I should really file assault charges," the attorney said, flustered, grabbing his briefcase off the table.

Sipowicz was straightening his tie, doing his Dangerfield neck and shoulder shrug. "Your client made a threatening movement. I took action."

Sinclair looked sharply at Fancy. Lieutenant?"

"I wasn't looking at your client," Fancy said. "Maybe he did make a threatening move. Would you like to file a complaint? Sort it out in front of a judge?"

A humorless laugh emanated from Sinclair's chest. "No. We'll let it pass, this time. But only this time. Do I make myself clear, Lieutenant? The harassment stops, or we're going to have a serious legal problem here."

Fancy rose, his chair scraping the floor, making Giardella flinch. "Thank you for coming in. We'll let you know if we have any further questions. You know the way out."

Sinclair shook his head disgustedly, nodded for Giardella to follow him. The mobster smirked at Sipowicz but didn't risk any further smart remarks.

When the attorney and client were gone, Fancy said, "That was stupid."

Sipowicz shrugged, avoided the Stonehenge stare of his boss. "So maybe I'm not a genius."

"Maybe. Stay within policy, Andy."

"Yeah. Sure."

Then the lieutenant surprised him. A very small, very white smile appeared in the dark face. "Pretty fast move."

Sipowicz was stunned for a second; then he grinned. "I used to play some ball as a kid. It was like slidin' into home."

Fancy's little smile faded and he headed for the door. Don't do that kind of thing again, Andy."

"Sure, Loo."

At the door Fancy paused. "Not in front of me. Or his lawyer."

And the lieutenant was gone.

"Not bad advice," Sipowicz said to himself.

It was end of shift now, and on the way out, Martinez stopped him and said, "How'd the interview go?"

"Up and down. The lieutenant seemed to feel my tryin' to strangle Giardella was maybe a procedural breach."

The kid grinned, lifted his eyebrows. "Wish I'd been there. You wanna grab a bite or somethin'?"

"What, back in Little Italy?"

"I was thinkin' Chinese."

"Naw. Thanks, kid. Maybe tomorrow."

"Okay. See ya then."

The kid waved and bounced off.

Sipowicz walked home as usual. He was amazed by how few times he'd thought about wanting a drink today. He was proud of himself. Maybe this was something he was finally getting a handle on. Maybe the light at the end of the tunnel wasn't a train.

So he stopped in at Patrick's to celebrate.

What could one little round hurt?

SEVEN

The day after his phone conversation with Frank O'Keefe, John Kelly—his arm in a sling but time and pain pills collaborating to help make him feel up to the effort—drove into the city to start his search for Honey Wayne.

He knew where *not* to begin. None of the current spate of New York City clubs—or their modern management, that morality-impaired mutt Giardella being a prime example—dated back to those more innocuous days of nightclubs and burlesque theatres; it was a long fall from the runways of Minsky's to the tawdry table dances of the Centerfold Lounge. The once-shocking but stagebound and safely distant bump-and-grind had been replaced by anonymous dry humps that would have outraged the likes of Gypsy Rose Lee and Ann Corio.

But Kelly knew of one business that thrived on keeping alive the radiant memories of Gypsy and Ann, not to mention Lile St. Cyr, Tempest Storm, and Blaze Starr. He and a friend of his, back in horny high school days, used to make regular weekend pilgrimages to East 14th and that second-floor mecca of cheesecake, Celebrity News.

Even now he could recall the fragrance of pulp paper, so important a part of the hypnotically musty bouquet of the twelve-by-twenty room crowded with bookshelves, file cabinets, stacked boxes; filled with old magazines, paperbacks, comic books, and eight-by-ten glossies of movie stars, pinup models, and strippers.

When he'd looked them up in the phone book, Kelly found Celebrity News listed on West 18th. Had they moved? Or had the temple of tease gone out of business, and had some new, less impertinent enterprise taken its sacred name, perhaps unknowingly?

If this Celebrity News was a public relations firm, he just might weep.

"Naw," the surprisingly young voice on the phone said, "we moved in eighty-four. It was gettin' cramped."

"You got anything on Honey Wayne?"

"The old stripper? Sure. She's a pretty hot ticket with the collectors."

"You don't say."

"Yeah, she hung around with gangsters. Like Candy Barr did with Mickey Cohen?"

"Really."

"Stuff's not cheap, though. Bring your plastic."

So he had trekked to West 18th, where he found a street-level store three times larger than the old location, but with the exception of wide aisles, every bit as jam-packed with pop-cultural bottom-feeding as ever.

About the only difference was that among the eight-by-tens displayed in plastic sleeves on the wall behind the cash register counter were—next to such genuine luminaries of pulchritude as Marilyn Monroe, Jayne Mansfield, Ann-Margret, and Raquel Welch—such dubious, more recent interlopers as Madonna, Sharon Stone, and Cindy Crawford. A display area of male stars had the audacity to place Tom Cruise and Brad Pitt in the same pantheon as Clark Gable and Gary Cooper. Civilization was definitely on the decline.

At the moment, late morning, business was sparse, and the clerk seemed glad for the company and was immediately chatty.

His name was Steve. Short, slender, average-looking, with a mustache as insubstantial as his dark thinning hair, he wore a black T-shirt that avertised the store—FIND ME AT CELEBRITY NEWS—over a line drawing of Marilyn Monroe in *The Seven Year Itch* skirt-blowing-up pose. Kelly made the guy at about thirty, bright-eyed, and enthusiastic, an eternal kid who got hired to work in a candy store.

"I used to come to the old location when I was a teenager," Kelly admitted, "and buy used *Playboys*."

"You're the guy I talked to on the phone," Steve said with a grin. "The Honey Wayne collector! I got a stack of stuff for ya."

And indeed he did. Old men's magazines from the fifties and early sixties—*Cabaret, Figure, Gala, Follies*. A few eight-by-tens, a couple of scandal magazines—*Confidential, Whisper*—with stories on the gangster and his stripper mistress: "The Moll and the Mobster," "The Girl and the Gun."

The "gun," Anthony Marino, was a darkly handsome Mafioso with a similar facial structure to his uncle Joe, and cold, dead eyes also similar to that contemporary *capo*.

The "girl," Honey Wayne, was a typical fifties blond bombshell, perhaps not as bosomy as others of her type, and not terribly leggy, with with a wasp waist that defined her hourglass shape, a dimpled behind, a heart-shaped face with large, luminous eyes, a pert nose, and lovely full lips.

And, of course, acres of honey-colored hair.

Could he blame his father if he'd fallen to the temptation of a beauty like this?

"The mags are individually marked," Steve was saying. "The ones with Honey Wayne covers are more, you'll notice."

They did seem a little excessive to him; these ancient skin mags with their fifty-cent and one-dollar cover prices now wore fifteen and twenty-buck tags on their plastic sleeves. The scandal mags, with their lurid black-and-white covers, were less—more in the eight-buck range.

"You take enough pieces," Steve said, "I can cut you a deal."

"You know," Kelly said, with an embarrassed little smile, "when I was buying old girlie mags, back in high school? I considered myself kind of an expert on this subject matter."

"Really."

"Yeah. For instance, Mamie Van Doren's real name was Joan Lucille Olander."

Steve, leaning on the counter, gave Kelly a narrow-eyed look. "Not bad. What about Stella Stevens?"

"Estelle Eggleston," Kelly said without hesitation.

"I'm impressed. You wouldn't wanna write for my mag, would you?"

"What mag would that be?"

Steve's smile was self-satisfied as he leaned forward to confide, "Managing this store is only my day job. In real life, I edit a fanzine called *Cheesecake International*. I also write for some of the big national magazines."

"Oh, yeah? Like what?"

He smirked proudly. "*Leg Tease* and *Juggs*."

Steve had carved himself out quite a career.

"Now *I'm* impressed," Kelly said. "But you know, it's a funny thing. Knowledgeable as I am about this stuff, I don't remember ever hearing of Honey Wayne."

Steve winced in confusion. "Then how come you're interested in her?"

"Somethin' I'm researchin'," Kelly said vaguely,

hoping not to have to show the guy his badge. This was personal.

"Well, these mags," Steve said, gesturing to a *Cabaret* with Honey depicted in a harem outfit, "they were lower-end product. Not so much color printing, ya know—and a little sleazier, with a blue-collar audience in mind. See, mags like *Playboy* and its imitators, *Escapade* and *Rogue* and those, you probably collected them . . . "

"Some," Kelly admitted.

"Well, they had this button-down, college-educated crowd that they served up that Hefner fantasy to—you know, the girl next door who just happens to be free-thinking, into beat poetry, and the proud owner of enormous bazooms."

"I get the picture," Kelly chuckled.

"So there was like this one buncha models, some of 'em starlets, even a few movie stars, some just figure models, who worked for those upper-scale skin mags. But these lower-end mags, they were servin' up a different fantasy. Harder-edged, more accessible girls. Lots of strippers, probably a few workin' girls. Ironically, Honey had probably the most wholesome image of any of these dames."

Funny hearing somebody in this day and age, particularly somebody no older than his early thirties, use the word "dames"—but appropriate in this musty titillation tabernacle.

Steve leaned across the counter and spoke in a conspiratorial whisper, even though the store was otherwise empty. "That's what makes Honey's bondage photos such a turn-on, even after all these years."

"Bondage photos?"

"Sure. Hell, man, that's what Celebrity News is famous for, didn't you know that?"

"No."

"Yeah, above the old store, there used to be a photo studio. Norma herself took the photos."

"Norma?"

"Sure! Harry's wife."

"Who's Harry?"

"Jeez, for a guy who knows Mamie Van Doren's real name, you got definite gaps in your education."

Steve explained, with patience and a know-it-all's delight, that Celebrity News had been founded by Harry Moscowitz back in the thirties; what had begun as a used book store had evolved into one of the country's first outlets for movie-star eight-by-tens.

In the early fifties, when movie stills depicting spanking and starlets tied in chairs and such proved the store's hottest ticket, Harry had set his wife up in a studio upstairs making specialty photos for a growing customer list.

"Not porn, you understand," Steve said. "No nudity. Just gals in Frederick's outfits tied to bedposts and into chairs and such. Nothin' much nastier than a Saturday matinee serial. And with Norma takin' the pictures, the girls were always at ease. She was like a den mother."

"I remember Norma," Kelly said. "I used to buy magazines from her."

His memory of Norma was of a very pleasant, very normal Jewish lady who had seemed old to him at the time, but who had probably only been in her forties.

Kelly sprang the question. "Whatever became of Honey Wayne?"

Steve shrugged. "That's the best-kept secret in cheesecake circles. I've tried to find her to do an article on her for my own 'zine. Nada luck. You know, she didn't do any modeling after around fifty-nine. She was actually a little older than a lot of the girls . . . some of these stills from her strip-circuit days date back to the forties."

"You have any idea how I could find her?"

"Forget about it. What I understand is, she got married, had a couple of kids, maybe found religion, and is very embarrassed about her modeling days. I mean, if you were a housewife in Schenectady, would you want the PTA knowin' you were some gangster's mistress and posed for bondage photos?"

Kelly leaned in. "Is that where she is? Schenectady?"

"That was just a hypothetical."

"It's important that I find her."

"Listen, are you gonna buy some magazines or not?"

"Is that what it's gonna take?"

"Hey, buy out the store, I still don't know where Honey Wayne is."

"Then where did you hear this housewife story?"

Steve shrugged. "I just heard it, is all."

"No. No. It was too specific."

Kelly dug out his wallet, flipped it open to show the shield there.

Now Steve was backing away, his eyes worried. "What, is this a police matter? You didn't say this was a police matter."

"Honey Wayne found Tony Marino dead. Somebody killed him with an ice pick."

"Are you kiddin'? That was a hundred years ago!"

"There's no statute of limitations on murder, Steve. Who do I talk to, to find Honey Wayne?"

"Who do you *think*? Norma . . . "

Norma Moscowitz.

"Where do I find her, Steve? Is she here? She have an office here?"

"She's got an office in back, but she's not here. She still comes in, but only twice a week, handlin' the mail order."

"Where does she live?"

"Long Island."

"She got a number?"

He shook his head no. "I'm not supposed to give it out."

Kelly put his free hand on Steve's shoulder; for a guy with his arm in a sling, he was pretty menacing. "You're remembering wrong, Steve. You're not supposed to *except* when it's a murder investigation."

"Oh . . . oh yeah."

"While you're writing down her address and number, Steve, I'll pick out some magazines."

"Okay."

Steve swallowed, got a pencil, and wrote on the back of a scrap of paper while Kelly sorted through the materials, taking both scandal rags, one of the stills, and three of the skin magazines.

The clerk handed Kelly the address and phone number, then used a calculator to total up the books.

"Comes to sixty-eight fifty before tax. How 'bout we make it sixty."

"Sixty even?"

"Naw," Steve said, "I gotta give the governor his share."

"I believe in paying taxes," Kelly said, getting out his Visa. "That's how public servants like me stay in business."

He took the paper sack of old magazines from the clerk. Then he gave the now-nervous contributor to big national magazines his hardest look.

"Don't call Norma about this, Steve," Kelly said. "Don't tell her I'm gonna be calling her."

"Then don't tell her I gave you her number," he said. "I need this gig."

"Done."

And John Kelly, for the first time in twenty years, left Celebrity News with a bag of dirty magazines under his arm.

When he returned home it was early afternoon, and as he moved in through the little foyer, past the kitchen, into the living room, golden sunshine filtering in their many windows, illuminating gracefully swimming dust motes, he realized he had company.

Sitting on the couch, feet tucked up under her, wearing a white terry bathrobe, a cup of coffee in hand, her face an immobile unreadable mask, was Laurie.

"Are you okay?" he asked with concern, setting the brown bag of magazines on the nearby coffee table. "You home sick?"

"No," she said, and the one syllable was like a bell tolling—for him. "I thought *you* were."

He made a little embarrassed facial shrug. "Yeah, well, I got stir crazy, and I was feeling better, so I went out for a while."

"I've been here for over two hours, John. Where have you been?"

He sat next to her, slipping out of the sling, which he tossed on the coffee table next to the paper bag. He touched her terrycloth-covered leg. "Not out cheatin' on ya, that's for sure."

His attempt at levity was leaden.

He tried another tack. "I wish you'd told me you were comin' home for the day."

"We talked about it. Remember? Maybe I'd take off a day and we'd spend a little time together working on 'natural remedies'?"

"I wish you'd called first."

She turned her gaze upon him; it was shriveling. Then each word came out with robotic precision: "I-wanted-to-surprise-you."

Well, she had.

"I'm sorry, Laurie." He shrugged, smiled, patted her leg. "The day's not over, ya know."

"You took the car. Where were you? What were you up to?"

"I went out to get something to read."

She leaned forward and took the sack from the table. "Let's see what took two hours to pick out."

"Laurie . . ."

She shook the old men's magazines out of the sack and looked at them with confusion and surprise, and finally, amusement. "If I'd known you were this horny, I'd have stayed home yesterday."

"Some collector's items I decided to pick up."

But now her expression darkened; her brow was knit as she said, "Honey Wayne . . . that's her, isn't it? The girl your father supposedly—"

"Yeah. Yeah."

She sighed, flopped the magazines down on the coffee table. It sounded like a slap.

"You're hopeless," she said. "Can't you let it lie?"

"No."

"What are you trying to do? Drive yourself crazy?"

"I don't know."

"Must you pick at your life like it's a scab? What are you trying to find out? How do you think you're going to look into some ancient murder, anyway?"

"I just have to know."

Her mouth tightened into a bitter line. "You have to know. What, are you losing it entirely? Johnny, some stupid remark by some mob asshole sends you burrowing into the past? Makes you question the reputation of a man beloved in the department? A man with a reputation you've devoted your life to living up to?"

Kelly got up and began to pace. "Don't you get it, Laurie? That's just it. I patterned my life on that man. Everything I am is built on that foundation."

"Yes, it is."

"And what if that foundation is false?"

"It's not false. Don't you know better than that?"

"Maybe I've been kidding myself. I thought my old man was the one man with integrity that New York City couldn't destroy. A stand-up guy, a cop's cop—"

"He was also a man, Johnny. A person. Maybe the 'foundation' had a crack in it—so what?"

"Laurie, if he covered up a murder—"

"What do you hope to accomplish with this?"

"I don't know."

"Come back over here and sit down."

He swallowed and did. She slipped her arm around his shoulder. "If you found out your father had covered up a murder, what would you do? Re-open the case?"

"I'm not doing this for the city. I'm doing this for me."

"What do you *hope* to find out?"

"I hope to find out that asshole Nardi was lying. That my dad didn't do this. That John Kelly, Sr., was not the kind of cop who covered up murders for strippers."

She took his hand, patted it. "Think it through. Let's take the worst-case scenario: Let's say your father did cover up this murder. Once you find out about it, if you choose not to tarnish his good name, and leave the murder covered up—which is what I would advise, incidentally—you have become what you fear your father may have been."

"But if he didn't do it . . . if there was no cover-up . . ."

"Let it alone, Johnny."

He shook his head. "I don't know if I can."

"Okay. What were you going to do next? What's your next step?"

He lifted the *Cabaret* with the Honey Wayne harem-girl cover. "Find her. Talk to her. She's still alive, you know."

Laurie's sigh was long and slow. "It was a long time ago. Don't you think she deserves her privacy?"

Funny—Laurie's instincts were so good; privacy, obscurity, that was exactly where Honey Wayne had gone. But had she gone there to hide? From a long-ago murder?

"I have a wonderful idea," Laurie said, and she uncinched the terrycloth robe. Her creamy rounded flesh beckoned to him. "You forget all about this nineteen-fifties sex bomb and spend some time with the woman who gave up an afternoon discussing variance applications and pension plans, just to be with her ailing husband."

She stood, leaving the robe behind, and walked toward the bedroom.

He left his own clothing in a trail behind him and they met in the bedroom, where she took the lead, getting astride him, putting no pressure at all on his wound. Afterward they slept, and made love again, and showered each other, and had a pizza delivered, and watched one of the movies she'd rented for him, and the subject of Honey Wayne never came up again.

He would wait until tomorrow morning, when Laurie was at work, to follow up the Norma Moscowitz lead.

EIGHT

S moke and mirrors.

That was a big part of how the Centerfold Lounge performed the magic act of turning its collection of young women into the flesh-and-blood fantasies gyrating on three circular, four-feet-off-the-floor stages: NYU students, single moms raising kids, green card cuties who'd traded in waitressing for a D-cup breast job, not to mention the occasional lovely lush or pretty junkie whose habits hadn't yet destroyed the still-young temples God gave them to live inside. Lighting—hot pink and cool blue, the lightning of strobes, the pooled glow of neon beer signs—further transformed the flawed, the ordinary, the human, into the perfect, the extraordinary, the superhuman, the living lust goddesses who inhabited the gritty unreality of this former mom-and-pop grocery.

The heavy metal rock blaring from high-mounted speakers provided the proper pulsating beat, and kept conversation to a minimum. Not that anyone was here to talk. Stale cigarette smoke and cheap perfume formed nostril-tickling slipstreams wafting through the hazy low-ceilinged chamber, mingling with the scent of hair spray and the aromas of sweat and body oils and lotions, creating just the otherworldly atmosphere its patrons craved.

Worshipping in this sanctuary of sleaze were men old and young, blue and button-down collar, executives, storekeepers, professors, waiters, guys who unloaded the backs of trucks; they wore jeans and suits, T-shirts and silk ties, sneakers and Italian loafers, and everything in between, some brazen, some embarrassed, with nothing in common but sin-shining eyes.

The only men in the room without that testosterone gleam were the bored bouncers, some black, some white, wearing ruffled tuxedo shirts over-stuffed with muscle, lurking on the perimeters like overdressed border guards.

On the center, slightly larger stage, a slender Hispanic with legs longer than an evening with an insurance salesman was wrapping herself, and those remarkable limbs, around the center stage pole, doing a snakelike slither in a blue sequined G-string.

At left, on one of the smaller stages, a slightly

chubby blonde with real breasts and a string-bikini bottom was watching herself in a wall mirror, ignoring the men waving dollars at her, ringside.

At right, a black girl—tall, limber, with a muscular dancer's body and an attractively close-cropped head—was flashing her whiter-than-white smile at the white males gazing up at her wide-eyed, coaxing their dollars into the sides of her sparkling amber G-string.

In New York City, an ordinance required the dancers cover their nipples, but the magic tape pasties these girls wore covered the letter of the law and nothing else.

Not that, had the dancers neglected wearing their pasties, Andy Sipowicz would've made the bust. So to speak.

It was four-thirty, give or take, and Sipowicz was on the job, but not on the clock. His tour of duty had been over at four, which was just the time the Centerfold employee he needed to speak with—one Shayna Lynn—began her shift.

According to Sid, the balding thirtyish tuxedoed manager of the joint, the young lady in question had been closer to the late Holly Jane Peterson than any of his other girls.

Sid—who smiled too much, whose eyes popped, and whose five o'clock shadow maade his face look smudged—knew all too well of Sipowicz's animosity toward Alfonse Giardella, Sid's boss. And, accordingly, the diminutive strip-club manager had been keeping his nose about a foot and a half up Sipowicz's ass, in apparent hopes that that animosity wouldn't rub off on him.

The girls at the Centerfold often broke the no-physical-contact rule when they table-danced, hoping to turn the ten-buck tariff into a twenty-spot or better. If a cop like Sipowicz spotted one of the girls rubbing her breasts in some lucky customer's face, and said cop felt like being a prick about it, the Centerfold lounge could face losing its liquor license.

So Sid had been helpful—maybe more helpful than his employer, Alfonse Giardella, would have liked. But what Al didn't know wouldn't hurt either of them, whereas if Sid lost the club's liquor license, Giardella's wrath would be considerable.

Sipowicz smirked to himself in his quiet corner of the room as he sipped the Scotch rocks. *Me and Sid,* he thought to himself, enjoying the free drink, *asshole buddies.*

"You want me to come along?" Martinez had asked, when Sipowicz casually mentioned he was stopping off at the Centerfold on his way home. They had spent the bulk of their day in Canarsie, checking out the friends and family of the missing Hotel Savory suspect, Sal Viana.

"It's Friday night," Sipowicz had said. "You tellin' me a kid like you don't have plans, Friday night?"

"Well, I'm not sayin' I don't have plans . . . "

"I don't need any help sittin' in a titty bar. This situation I can handle without a partner."

Martinez had grinned a little. "You sure about that?"

"There's not some remark about my age you were thinking about offering?"

"The grin remained. "No, no." Then it faded. "But you're gonna try to talk to this Shayna Lynn, right?"

Shayna Lynn was the only Centerfold Lounge employee they had not been able to interview. She hadn't been in to work since her friend Holly had been murdered; too grief-stricken, she'd told the club manager.

"Yeah, my new best friend, Sid, over at our favorite adult entertainment establishment," Sipowicz said, "called and said she's comin' in tonight. I figure maybe I'll strike up a conversation."

"You want company, you got it," Martinez tried again.

"No, thanks. Why don't you go out and find some woman who, if she takes her blouse off, you don't have to tip her."

Why hadn't he wanted the kid along? Sipowicz wasn't sure himself. But maybe it had to do with the heavy drinking he had every intention of doing here at the Centerfold. This kid seemed to look up to him, and Sipowicz didn't feel like disillusioning him so early in the game.

Sooner or later, Martinez—like all of Andy Sipowicz's friends—would find out what a charming drunk he made.

The Hispanic babe stepped down from center-stage, replacing the chubby, busty, self-absorbed dancer at left, who disappeared into the forbidden recesses of the club, the no-man's-land of dressing/locker rooms.

The heavy metal tune faded and the percolator-like rhythms and heartbeat undercurrent of a disco-tinged oldie—"Heart of Glass"—came blasting out of the speakers.

The male D.J.—who constantly chattered a steady stream of sophomoric innuendo no one listened to, except when he was introducing the next girl, which is what he was doing now—said, "And now, direct from Las Vegas, straight from the pages of *High Society* magazine, the Centerfold Lounge's favorite natch-ur-al blond—*Shay*-nah!"

She was tiny and blond with big *Baywatch* hair, her compact, curvy, perfectly proportioned body easily discernible through the sheer red teddy; she wore a candy-apple-red bra and matching panties beneath the lingerie, and her spike heels were red, too, as red as the lipstick of her generous, sexy/puffy mouth. Her eyes were huge and china-blue and her nose was pug; her heart-shaped face gave her a vague resemblance to Debbie Harry, which perhaps explained her somewhat dated choice of background music.

She didn't dance, exactly; right now she was just strutting, smiling at the men crowding the stage, sitting forward in their chairs, dollars ready (they wouldn't release those dollars till clothing began to drop). She'd wave at them, giggle at them. Fresh, little girlish. Quite a convincing act.

When the next song came around—"Touch Me,"

an orgasmic anthem that was newer than "Heart of Glass" but not exactly a recent chart-topper, either—she lost the teddy, and gained a shower of wadded-up dollars, flung enthusiastically at her feet. She still wasn't dancing, really, just walking around in time to the disco-ish beat, flirting with the men, waving at them, driving them nuts.

Sipowicz shifted in his seat. She was good, this kid; anyway, she was getting a rise out of him.

Finally, another relative oldie came up—"I Touch Myself"—and the bra went away, leaving her nice natural B-cups exposed but for their transparent pasties, and she stepped out of the panties, too, unveiling a G-string that revealed a perfectly rounded behind, and in front a trail of fuzzy blond baby hair that disappeared into her G-string.

Sipowicz hailed a waitress down for another Scotch.

Then the little blonde under the flickering lights got dreamy and she cupped her breasts and touched the cheeks of her ass, and then slapped them and grinned with innocent evil. She hung on the center-stage shaft like it was a Maypole, twirling around it like a kid, with no dancer's grace at all but still utterly beguiling.

Finally she began going around the stage, climbing down to spend a little time with each of her fans, who stuffed dollar bills—and a few five-spots—into the sides of her G-string. She would touch their cheeks, give them little pecks of kisses on their foreheads, make each of them feel special.

Then her song was over, and she got a big round
of applause and whistles and hoots before she gath-
ered her discarded teddy and bikini and the crumpled
dollars, and moved over to the stage at right.

Shayna worked both of the smaller stages without
taking anything away from the star of the moment.
First, it was a medley of Z.Z. Top and a fringe-vest
and cowboy-hat wearing, carrot-topped girl with good
cheekbones and a very rigid-looking silicone pair.
Then it was back to heavy metal for a skinny black-
leather-jacket and mesh-stocking dressed brunette
with an angelic face, nose ring, and biker tattoos.

When a girl was done, she sometimes went back
to the dressing room, other times taking advantage of
the momentum she'd built up with customers by
starting in on the table dances she'd booked while
working the three stages.

That was what Shayna did, and she worked
through the next three sets without a break. Finally,
still cheerful and energetic, she had run out of
customers and was heading for the back when Sipowicz called out to her.

She grinned at him and came over. "Guess I got
time for another." The music had already started—
more heavy metal—so she said, "Why don't we sit
this out, and do the next one? I can catch my breath,
and you can get your money's worth."

"Look, I don't want a table dance."

Her friendly expression turned blank—not hostile,
just empty. "Oh. Well . . . if we're just gonna talk,
you gotta buy me a drink. Honest, mister, it's a

better deal, and I make out better, if you take a table dance—"

"Maybe later. Right now, how about we just talk?"

She shrugged. "Fine."

He offered his hand. "My name's Andy."

She took it, shook it, and her smile seemed genuine. "Hi, Andy. I'm Shayna."

"Hi, Shayna," He smiled nervously. "What made you pick those songs you danced to? Aren't they a little before your time?"

She shrugged. "I like classic rock."

"Classic rock?"

"Oh, yeah! My mom was a big Blondie fan. Samantha Fox, I remember hearing her on the radio, when I was little."

Suddenly he felt ancient. Of course, it wasn't the first time.

"I notice," he said, trying to be conversational, "you got varied styles of music here, that you young ladies, uh . . . perform to."

She nodded. "When you take center stage," she said, "the song choice is yours. I mean, it's *your* act, after all."

"And the girls on the side stages are just kinda stuck with your selection, huh?"

"Sure. But I like the variety. There's one girl who does all fifties songs, Elvis, Buddy Holly, 'Mack the Knife.' "

She looked around, a little puzzled apparently, by why no waitress had come scurrying around yet.

"You know, Andy, you're going to have to buy me

a drink. You seem like a nice guy, but, you know, a girl's gotta make a living, and I'll get in trouble if—"

"Lou's not gonna stiff me for any drinks. I'm on the cuff, anyway."

"Really! What, are you a cop or something?"

"Yes."

Her eyes widened. They were the lightest blue he'd ever seen; and were filigreed red, indicating some recent crying jags, despite her perky, cheery demeanor. Close-up, this girl was still lovely; a little bit of a complexion problem, under all that makeup. But lovely.

"I don't wanna spook anybody and take out my badge or anything," he said. Then he dug in his pocket. "Here's my card, though. That do it for ya?"

She took it, looked at it, put it on the table before her, shrugged a little. "Okay."

"I been leavin' messages, tryin' to talk to you, for the last couple days, you know."

She swallowed. "About Holly."

"That's right."

She lowered her gaze. "She was my best friend. She was like a second mom to me."

"I'm sorry for your loss."

"It was horrible. I wouldn'ta come in, today, but . . . you know. Friday's a good money day. You know, we don't get anything but tips, so I just couldn't afford not to come in.

He shrugged. "Probably best to get your mind off it, anyway."

"Yeah." She looked at him searchingly. "Are you just pretending to be nice? Or are you *really* nice?"

Something about this kid melted him, and he felt himself smile and heard himself say, "I'm a big teddy bear."

Of course, a few more Scotches and he might unholster his revolver and start shooting up the joint; but right now, Sipowicz was in his warm and fuzzy stage. The inevitable mindless rage came later.

"I *collect* teddy bears," she oozed. "You know . . . there's things I wanna tell you about Holly." She leaned close to him; her perfume was pleasant but overpowering—she must have bathed in the stuff. "I don't feel comfortable, talking about it here."

"Where can we go?"

"I work till ten. Sometimes I catch some breakfast, at the Sportspage, you know? You wanna get together, after?"

"Sure."

"You wanna come back, or stick around?"

Sipowicz shrugged. "I'll stick around." He gave her a little smile. "Maybe I'll even spring for a table dance."

Her smile was pure innocence. "I can make life hard for you."

Then she was off to the dressing room.

In a corner booth of the Sportspage, in the smoking section, Sipowicz sat across from Shayna, who looked remarkably different. The big hair had been a wig— her real hair was short and spiky, though just as blond—and she wore no makeup, except for some zit touch-up on the places around her mouth where she was broken out a little. She wore a T-shirt with a sixties movie poster on it—*Faster Pussycat, Kill Kill*—flea-market jewelry, and jeans that had holes in the knees.

She looked about fourteen.

She was smoking one of Andy's cigarettes. They'd had breakfast—she had eggs and bacon and greasy hash browns, the sort of high-cholesterol time bomb only the young dared in good conscience consume, and he had the same.

He was smoking a cigarette, too.

So far it has been small talk. She was from the Midwest—didn't say where. She wanted to be a movie star—came to New York because she heard it was better to start out on the stage.

"Tell me about Holly," he said finally.

"She was just the greatest. The sweetest. She was getting out of the biz, you know."

"Really."

She waved a cigarette-in-hand theatrically, trailing smoke. "Yeah. She was old, really old."

Twenty-eight.

"How old are you, Shayna?"

"Nineteen." She shrugged. "I look younger. That's why I make out so good on tips. Older men, they go for young girls. Holly said it was the 'implied incest thing.' "

"Did she, now?"

"Yeah. She was real smart. She went to college. I don't think she graduated, but she went."

"Did you know about her boyfriend?"

"Lou? Sure. I met him, before. What a sweet guy."

"Yeah. He was a saint."

"You knew him?"

"We were acquainted. Shayna—did you know Lou Nardi was a witness in a court case?"

"Sure. He and Holly were goin' into the Witness Protection Plan together."

He leaned forward, kept his voice down. "Shayna, how many of the girls at the club knew this?"

She shrugged. "None. Just me. We were close. We had a bond. I told you, she was like a mom to me."

"Did you mention this to anybody?"

"Mention what?"

"This Witness Protection Plan aspect."

"No. Of course not."

"Are you sure?"

"Andy, you're starting to sound like a cop."

He reached across and gripped her wrist. "Are you *sure*?"

She pulled her wrist away. "That hurt. That wasn't nice. And, yes, I'm sure. Ouch."

" 'Cause if you did . . . "

Her eyes widened. "Oh. You're saying . . . I could've caused what happened to her. . . ."

He nodded gravely.

"Andy, I swear, I never said a word. I don't have

any other friends at the club; Holly, she kinda took me under her wing. She talked to me about drugs and things like that."

"Talked to you how? What was was her stand on the drug issue, exactly?"

"Against."

Well, maybe Holly *had* been like a mom to Shayna.

Suddenly he felt ashamed of himself. "I didn't mean to hurt you, there . . ."

She was rubbing her wrist. She shrugged. "It's all right. I know you didn't mean it."

"Listen, Shayna—what makes you like me, anyway? Is it my imagination, or . . ."

"You remind me of somebody, that's all."

"Oh. Old boyfriend?"

"Something like that. Are you going to find out who killed Holly?"

"I know who killed her. I mean—I know who had it done."

The china-blues were huge. "Who?"

"Your fat-ass boss."

"Lou? He isn't fat—"

"Alfonse Giardella."

Another theatrical wave of the cigarette. "Oh. Mr. Giardella. But that's impossible."

"Why?"

She smiled, shook her head, as if he were being silly. "Mr. Giardella liked Holly. They were friends. Have you ever met Mr. Giardella?"

"We've met on occasions."

She flounced a wrist, breathed smoke out dragon-like through her nostrils. "Well, he's the sweetest man. He's been such a help to my career."

"Really?"

"Oh, yes. He's a movie producer, you know."

"Yeah, I do know."

And Sipowicz knew what kind of movies.

"Listen, Shayna—the night Holly was killed, did you see anything suspicious, anything . . ."

Her pretty features tightened with concern that seemed genuine. "Oh, Andy. I wish I could help. But I didn't work the night Holly was . . . the night she died."

Shit.

"Andy—you look . . . disappointed?"

He was stabbing his cigarette out in a glass ash-tray. "That's the word for it."

"You were . . . hoping . . . hoping I'd lead you to something, weren't you?"

"Yeah. Look, I better pay for this. I need a drink."

She brightened at this change of topic. "What do you like?"

"I like Scotch. Bourbon. The list goes on."

"What would you . . . nothing."

"What, Shayna?"

"I have some wine at my apartment. It's not far from here. Over on Fourth."

"Wine makes me sleepy."

She shrugged. Smiled. "I have a bed."

Sipowicz stared at the fresh lovely face. Hell, she didn't look fourteen, she looked *twelve*—except for those kittens fighting under that T-shirt.

"Just let me take care of this," he said, picking up the check.

NINE

Mid-morning Friday, Kelly—arm still in a sling, but time and pain pills keeping him on top of his game—drove out to Long Island to see Norma Moscowitz.

It was just forty minutes on the expressway, and a pleasant drive, fairly light traffic on this perfect sunny day. Mrs. Moscowitz lived in Port Jefferson, an area with some money to be sure; she lived just past the marina. As he neared her neighborhood, the sparkling expanse of water on his left was decorated with yachts and smaller craft. This was a much different world than either of the neighborhoods that had housed the Moscowitz retail business, Celebrity News.

She lived in a little white Cape Cod in a well-tended, upper middle-class neighborhood of mostly older people; even in the summer there was no sound of children playing, and only the occasional yapping dog. The lawns looked like golf greens, and driveways harbored land yachts.

He had spoken to her on the phone this morning.

"My name is Kelly, Mrs. Moscowitz," he'd said.

"I don't believe I know you, Mr. Kelly," a no-nonsense voice replied, with little or no elderly quaver, "and I don't accept phone solicitations."

"I used to be a customer of yours, when I was in high school."

"I'm afraid that doesn't narrow it down, Mr. Kelly. A lot of boys came into the shop. Still do."

"I'm a detective now, with the Fifteenth Precinct in Manhattan—"

"My store isn't in that precinct."

"I know—"

"Is there a problem? Is there trouble?"

He was going at this badly.

"No, Mrs. Moscowitz," he said. "But I have a few questions I need to ask you, about a police matter. Could I drive out to speak with you this morning? Will you be home?"

"I'll be home," she said. "But what sort of police matter are we talking about here?"

"I'd rather not discuss this over the phone. I'll be out within the hour, if that's convenient."

"Well . . . I'll be working on my roses."

And she was, kneeling at the bushes at the base of her porch, pruning the gloriously red roses.

He had left his dark blue sedan at the curb and

crossed the S-winding walk, and now ventured onto the flawless lawn, moving over by where she was snipping the little heads off the dead flowers among the living, leaving the survivors more room to flourish.

She glanced up at him from under a straw sunbonnet that was smaller than a flying saucer. She wore jeweled sunglasses that had been in fashion perhaps forty years ago, but otherwise she looked crisply modern—white short-sleeved blouse, light blue slacks, cream-color tennies. The big yellow gardening gloves on the end of dark slender arms were like the hands of an animated cartoon character, Goofy hands. Her elongated face was (despite the hat) deeply tanned, leathery, every character line of seventy years distinct and hard-earned.

"I remember you," she said. She smiled just a little, like somebody was lightly tickling her and she was resisting. "Jimmy. *Playboys.*"

"It's Johnny, Mrs. Moscowitz. Detective John Kelly."

She snipped the head off another dead rose, then stood. She stared at him with the big blank eyes of her sunglasses. "You're a policeman, now. Not vice cop, I hope."

He grinned. "No. No. Not vice cop."

She nodded toward his sling. "What happened to your arm?"

"I got shot the other day."

"Really?"

"Really."

She returned to her snipping. "I hope you won't be too uncomfortable, talking out here. Sit on one of the steps, if you like."

"No, I'm fine."

"I'd invite you in, but things are a bit untidy inside. I had the grandchildren all week, till yesterday, and my cleaning help doesn't come till this afternoon."

"This shouldn't take that long."

"I really don't mean to be rude, Jimmy."

"Johnny. John. Mrs. Moscowitz, I'm trying to locate a witness in a murder case."

She whipped the sunglasses off; her eyes were large and brown, within age-deepened sockets—and alarmed. "A *murder* case?"

"It's a very old case, Mrs. Moscowitz. But it *is* unsolved, and—"

Now the eyes narrowed with the shrewdness that had kept her in business all these years. "Kelly, you said?"

"John Kelly, yes, that's right—"

Her expression froze at the sound of the name, a name he'd given her before but which hadn't caught her attention, apparently. Now it had: her eyes were glazed, either looking past him or through him. Then, with a very conscious effort, she searched his face, her eyes landing on his red hair.

"My God, but you look like him," she said, and it was as if he'd hit her in the stomach with a fist. She weaved, and he helped her, taking her arm. She moved toward the steps, he continued guiding her, and she sat on a step while he stood and waited for her to compose herself.

"You're John Kelly's son?" she said, and the strong voice seemed weak now.

"Yes. I'm John Kelly's son."

Her head was lowered; with the large sunbonnet blocking the way, he couldn't see her face. And her voice was distant.

"He was a handsome man, your father."

"I know."

"More handsome than you."

"I know that, too."

She peeked up from under the bonnet at him. "Not that you're a bad-looking young man."

"Mrs. Moscowitz—"

"Norma." She sighed, and removed her bonnet with a sweep of the hand, as if taking a bow. "You know I always insisted my customers call me Norma."

"Norma. I'm looking for Honey Wayne."

She said nothing. She was staring past him again—not so glazed now, in fact not glazed at all; more of a reflective stare.

"What do you know about my father and Honey Wayne?"

She shrugged. "I don't really know anything, except that they were friends."

"Friends? Or were they more than friends, Norma?"

She brought her gaze up to his face and she frowned. "Is that your business, young man?"

"He was my father."

"That doesn't make his personal life your business, now, does it?" The frown lines deepened in the leathery face. "And I thought this was a police matter."

"Tony Marino was murdered. Stabbed to death with an ice pick."

Another shrug. "Centuries ago."

"It's an open case on the books, Norma."

The half-smile that made a crevice in her cheek was part amused, part confused. "And you want to solve it? Or just poke around in your father's dirty laundry?"

"Does he have dirty laundry, Norma? My father?"

She was looking past him again. "He was a hand-some man. And, oh, she was a beauty. Honey hair and an hourglass figure. You didn't collect her, did you, Jimmy? Before your time. But a beautiful girl. Beautiful. They busted us, once."

"Who did?"

"Postal authorities. Those mild little bondage things we did, such a fuss. Honey testified."

"Where?"

"Kefauver hearings. They asked her questions about pornography. Can you imagine? Those mild little pictures I took. Spanking. Bras and panties and stockings and a little rope. G-rated now, they'd be."

"Did she testify about Tony Marino?"

"They asked her about him, too. You know, that's how he met Honey."

"Pardon?"

"Tony Marino. He was one of my best customers."

"For bondage photos, you mean?"

She nodded. "He had specific requests, and we'd have the girls do them. We shot some . . . private photos. A little naughtier."

He narrowed his gaze at her. "Would those photos be G-rated today, Norma?"

She shrugged. "Maybe R. Anyway, they were private. Personal. Some things are, you know."

"Some things are what?"

"Private. Personal."

He sat on the step next to her. Looked over at her. Kept his voice quiet. Gentle. "Norma, I want to talk to Honey Wayne."

"Are you going to re-open the case?"

"No."

"Then this isn't really a police matter, is it?"

"No," he admitted.

"It's personal," she said.

"Some things are."

"Maybe it should stay private, too."

"I'd like to talk to Honey Wayne. Is she still alive?"

"If I said she wasn't, would you believe me?"

"No."

"What would you do?"

"I'd keep looking."

"And you'd find her, wouldn't you?"

"That's right. I'm a detective. If I want to find her, she can't hide from me."

"It's not you she's hiding from."

"What is she hiding from, Norma?"

"What we're all hiding from, Jimmy. The things in the past that we wish hadn't happened."

Someone was mowing a lawn down the street. A dog barked. An American flag flapped on some patriotic neighbor's pole.

He put his hand on the withered, leathery flesh of her skinny arm, just above the Goofy glove. "Will you help me, Norma? Will you tell me where she is?"

Norma Moscowitz sighed, nodded. "Yes."

Within him, he felt a collapsing feeling; his emotions were sending him mixed signals. He had gotten the answer he so desired, and so dreaded.

"You want to know why I'm going to tell you?"

"Only if you want to tell me, Norma."

"Lots of people have asked me whatever happened to Honey Wayne? Media people. TV shows. Offered me money, good money, and I told 'em to go peddle their papers."

"I'm glad you decided to help me, Norma."

"Know why?" She was smiling a crinkly little smile. "I think she'd like to look at that Irish mug of yours. I think she'd like to know that something lives on of John Kelly. He was shot, wasn't he?"

"Yes."

"A young man."

Kelly nodded. "Not all that much older than I am now."

"You love your father?"

"Very much."

"Then take an old woman's advice: walk away."

"No, thanks."

"Your father was stubborn, too, you know." She stood, plucking off the cartoon gloves. "Wait here—I'll go in and get the address out of my book, write it down for you. Did Steve at the store give you my number?"

"No," Kelly lied.

"It's unlisted, but then you cops can find things out, can't you?"

"That's what we do."

"So I shouldn't tear Steve a new asshole."

"I wouldn't, no."

She shrugged, went inside, and came back about four minutes later and handed him a slip of paper with the address: a retirement home in New Paltz.

"Don't tell her I gave you this," she said.

"Don't tell her I'm coming," he said.

"I won't if you won't."

"Deal," he said with a shrug.

She was kneeling at her rose bushes again when he walked back to the car; but she wasn't snipping.

Just staring.

Staring.

When Laura got home that night, he met her at the door. He could tell instantly she was pissed. Her jaw was firm, and there was no love in the husky voice when she said, "Where were you?"

He followed her into the kitchen. "Where was I when?"

"The three times I called this morning."

He shrugged. "I was here all afternoon."

She slipped out of her suit jacket, flipped it on the back of a chair. "That wasn't what I asked."

"I just meant, I was here all afternoon, and you didn't call."

Her back was to him; she was getting a packet of instant cappuccino out of the cupboard. "I was in court."

"Oh, yeah, you had that thing with the building permits."

"Right." She turned to look at him. "Where were you this morning?"

He sat at the table. He was out of the sling—anyway, his arm was. His ass was apparently back in.

"Jeez, Laurie, it's like you think I'm havin' an affair or somethin'."

She filled a coffee cup with tap water, put it in the microwave. "You want anything?"

"No, thanks. You know I'm not havin' an affair, right?"

"Right."

"So what do you *think* I'm doin'?"

She shut the microwave door—slammed it, actually. "What you said you wouldn't: you're looking for that old stripper of your father's."

He winced. "I wish you wouldn't put it that way."

"Isn't that where you were?"

"Actually, yes. I went out to Long Island and saw this woman that Honey Wayne used to work for."

The microwave buzzed and Laurie removed the cup, emptied a packet of Caffe D'Amore into the cup, stirred. "You just can't leave it alone, can you?"

"Laurie, I don't remember telling you I was going to stop looking into this."

"You implied it."

He shrugged. "I don't think that would hold up in court, but you're the lawyer."

Laurie sat at the table with her cappuccino, a question mark of smoke twirling out of it. "So, have you found her?"

"I have her address."

Her smile was ironic and not at all nice. "And you haven't gone to see her yet? Such willpower."

"It's a bit of a drive."

She sipped, frowned. "Where?"

"New Paltz."

"Really. What's an old stripper doing in New Paltz?"

"Living in a retirement home."

Her laugh was as short as it was humorless. "Living in a retirement home. And you want to go bother her about some bygone crime, and try to figure out if your father cheated on your mother."

Kelly shook his head no. "I don't think he was married to Mom yet, when he knew Honey Wayne. Engaged, maybe."

"Then why do you care if he slept with her or not?"

"Did I say I did?"

Now Laurie was shaking her head. "There's something sick about this, John."

"*You* make it sound that way."

"Then what *is* this about?"

His mouth twitched before he found the words to say, "It's about . . . about whether or not my father . . . whether he covered up this murder or not."

She looked at him, not without sympathy, for several long moments before she spoke.

"If he did, if he covered up some crime because he loved the woman who committed it, or maybe committed it himself, to protect her, what would that mean, Johnny? Would you not love him any-more? Would you not respect his memory? Would you quit the force?"

He turned away from her gaze. "I don't like where this is going."

"Me, either." She did something with her mouth that was partly a smile, partly a grimace. "So, tomor-row . . . we were supposed to go to that flea market, remember? Or are you too sick?"

"I'm going to New Paltz."

"What a surprise."

"You want to come along? You know, it's a pretty drive this time of year."

She rolled her eyes, and her laugh sounded hollow. "Oh, fine. We'll make an *outing* of it!"

"Stay home, then. I don't really give a damn."

She sipped at the cup. Her eyes looked moist. "What I say doesn't matter. My opinion is, what? Just the little woman grousing?"

"That's not fair."

"I'll go with you. But I won't go in. I'll keep you company, on the ride. But I won't help you go snooping around sniffing bedpans at some retirement home, bothering old people."

Now he studied her for a while, before speaking.

"Why, Laurie? I mean—you're against this. Why go along at all?"

"You're still my husband," she said. "And I love you."

"I love you, too, Laurie."

"That's never been a problem, has it?"

"What?"

"Loving each other. It's the living that gives us fits." She stood, carried the cup to the sink, rinsed it out. Sighed. "Hard day. I think I'm going to take a shower."

He gave her his best impish smile. "There's an idea."

"Alone, Johnny," she said, in a tone as flatly expressionless as her face, and she left the kitchen.

TEN

A slash of sun from around the drawn shade cut across Sipowicz's eyes, wounding them open. He winced, swore, and turned away, and was suddenly staring into a button-eyed, fuzzy brown face.

This startled him fully awake, more or less, in bed—a twin bed—and found himself splayed out on top of a pink frilly spread, surrounded by teddy bears, small, large, in-between, some wearing cute little costumes.

This was not Andy Sipowicz's bedroom.

In T-shirt and boxer shorts, he sat up, making the bed squeak, and rubbed his forehead; his tongue was a thick fuzzy tumor, his head a skull-contained explosion.

The ancient plaster walls were painted hot pink, which didn't hurt his eyes any more than staring at the sun, and decorated with posters of contemporary movie and pop stars, Madonna and other current blond bimbos and various puffy-lipped gay-looking hunks, none of whose names Sipowicz had ever bothered to commit to memory.

He sat on the edge of the bed, rubbing his eyes with the heels of his hands. He was in his black socks; all he lacked for a role in an old smoker loop was the mask.

Hot pink walls or not, he took in the little room. A blond-colored art-deco dresser from the forties that would have been a valuable collector's item if it weren't scarred and veneer-chipped was littered with perfume, makeup, and jewelry. Snapshots ringed the mirror. A metal garment rack against one wall was teaming with sexy apparel—a little cheerleader's outfit, mini-skirts, hot pants, halters, lingerie, black leather bras and panties, a few slinky sequined gowns, feather boas . . . stripper stuff.

The punk-haired Shayna peeked in. She was wearing a long white T-shirt with a kitty on it; the shirt came to her knees.

"You're awake, finally," she said.

"Technically," he said. "What time is it?"

"You don't have to go to work, do you? Last night you said you didn't have to go to work today, but I wasn't sure if I should believe you."

"Not a bad piece of judgment on your part," he said. "But, no—I don't go in today."

"It's nine-thirty-something," she said, finally answering his question. She came over and sat on the little seat by her dressing table; she leaned forward, sitting knock-kneed. In no makeup, she was more cute than pretty, except for the big beautiful china-blue eyes, and looked very young.

A little too young—especially considering Sipowicz had no memory of this bedroom, and only the vaguest recollection of the videotape-cluttered living room where she'd poured him wine and talked of her love of movies.

"How old did you say you were, Shayna?"

"Nineteen. You want some breakfast?"

He touched his Buddha belly, belched behind a fist, then said, "No. I'll just keep workin' on that one I had last night. Listin, uh . . . last night . . ."

"Don't worry about it," she said.

"Don't worry about what?"

She flounced a hand in the air. "The lamp. It wasn't an antique or anything."

"I busted a lamp?"

She seemed embarrassed. "Yeah. A little."

He lifted his eyebrows, rolled his eyes. "Jeez, I'm sorry. I sometimes get sorta . . . you know, belligerent, when I overindulge. I didn't . . . uh, hit you or anything? Not that I have a history of that—"

"No," she said, shaking her head. "Strictly verbal."

"What made me get mad?"

Her eyes swept the wooden floor. She looked about fourteen. "I don't wanna talk about it. You might just get mad again."

It was something about movies . . . how she was going to be a star and—"

"You made a porno," he said.

She shrugged. "That's an ugly word."

His laugh was humorless. "Oh, what—are we in the erotica area here? The world of art films? It's triple-X smut, Shayna. What are ya gettin' involved in that kinda thing for, nice kid like you? You don't get Oscars from that shit—you get AIDS!"

She swallowed. "You sound like Holly."

"Your late friend."

And Lou "The Lover" Nardi's last love. . . .

Shayna nodded.

Sipowicz said, "Holly, she didn't approve of this . . . 'acting' endeavor, either."

She shrugged, then nodded again. "I didn't tell her. I mean, I told her I was thinking about doing it, and she had a *cow* about it, so I . . . I lied to her."

"You told her you'd decided against it."

Another shrug, another nod.

"But then you went ahead and did it, anyway."

"Sure. It was a big break. I had the *lead*."

"You like having sex with strangers on film?"

"It was just two guys, and they were cute and real clean. Anyway, it wasn't film. It was video."

"Well, that makes all the difference."

"You're trying to make me feel bad."

"How did humping for the camera make you feel?"

Now she began to cry.

"Shit," he said. He stumbled over to her, an overweight, alcoholic, desperately hungover cop in his T-shirt, shorts, and socks, giving a kid advice on how to live a better life.

He put his arm around her, gently; nothing even remotely sexual in the gesture. Patted her. "You just do that. Cry awhile."

She buried her head in his shoulder and sobbed.

"I . . . I . . . I . . ."

She sounded like Medavoy.

"I . . . I miss Holly."

"Sure you do. She was your friend."

"She was like my mom, only better."

"Sure."

She looked up with big wet china-blue eyes. "You think I let her down? Doing that video?"

"I think you let yourself down. You're better than that. Jeez, honey—you don't do drugs, do you?"

"No. I smoke. Cigarettes, I mean. But no dope at all. It's bad for you."

"That's right. Do you drink much?"

"Hardly at all. Just a little wine."

"Well, that's a good practice. You saw me last night, didn't you? That's what can happen when drinking gets out of hand."

She was looking at him with surprising, heartbreaking fondness. "You weren't so bad."

He shook his head. "What's a kid like you, whose worst habit is keeping one-day rental videos over the weekend, doin' prostituting herself?"

She reared back, frowning, and her tone was defensive. "Being in an adult film isn't prostitution."

"It's sex for money. Don't kid yourself. What do you make a week at the Centerfold?"

She shrugged. "A thousand, fifteen hundred. Depends."

Kind of hard advising a kid like this to give that up for waitressing.

"So you can't scrape by on that?" Sipowicz asked. "You gotta have extra income from this pornography crap?"

She was moving her head, side to side, like Stevie Wonder singing; she was trying to reason with him. "It wasn't the money. The money was . . . it wasn't so much, a thousand a day, for three days."

He decided not to tell her how good that money sounded.

"Then what was it, Shayna?"

She grabbed air with both hands and the hands became little fists. "It was the chance to star in a movie! Mr. Giardella says I have a big future—"

"Giardella." Sipowicz grunted a laugh. "*He's* the star maker, here."

"He's been wonderful to me."

"Tell me, honey—what was your friend Holly's opinion of your patron saint Alfonse?"

"Well . . . "

"She thought he was poison, didn't she?"

She looked away from him. "Yeah. I guess so. But she was biased."

"Biased?"

Now she looked back at him. "Yeah. You know—

because her boyfriend Lou and Mr. Giardella had that falling out. Over business."

"Business." He leaned forward. "Do you read the papers, Shayna?"

"Not that much. My horoscope, sometimes."

"Are you aware that Holly's boyfriend Lou got himself killed, the same day she did?"

She was looking away again. But she nodded.

"And did it occur to you there might be a relationship between those two events, Lou getting whacked and what happened to Holly?"

"I guess. Sure."

"And you *still* think Mr. Giardella is wonderful?"

She frowned. "Lou was testifying against all kinds of big gangsters, is what I heard. What makes you think Mr. Giardella did that?"

"I read his horoscope for the day. It said it was a good day for him to hire a low-life hitman to wipe out a scumbag ex-business partner."

"You're making fun of me." She smirked poutily, then shrugged it off. "Anyway, those gangsters are always killing each other."

"So then you acknowledge that Mr. Giardella is a gangster?"

She shrugged again. "I guess."

"Who do you think is responsible for Holly's murder?"

"Not Mr. Giardella."

"Yes Mr. Giardella. Don't lie to yourself. That's a habit right in there with drugs and booze."

Her mouth was tight, her whole face was tight, as she bit off the words: "He's gonna make me a star."

"By having sex on camera?"

"He says a lot of girls are . . . making the transition. Crossing over. You ever hear of Ginger Lynn Allen? Traci Lords?"

"I heard Traci Lords was underage when she made her—"

And something passed across the girl's face, like a cloud turning a sunny day into shadows. He looked carefully at her, and she turned away.

Suddenly there was a very sick feeling at the bottom of his stomach.

He moved away from her, sat on the edge of the bed again, right across from her, and looked at her. Hard.

"Shayna . . . what's your *real* name, anyway?"

Matter-of-factly, but still not looking at him, she said, "It is Shayna, but my last name isn't Lynn. It's Marshek. Ugly name."

To a guy named Sipowicz, Marshek sounded like sheer poetry.

"Shayna . . . last night . . . did we, did I . . . " He patted the bed with tenderness and terror. "Did we have relations?"

Now she looked at him, surprised, amused. "No. You were a perfect gentleman. You broke the lamp, and stumbled in here and fell asleep."

Thank God.

"I slept on the couch," she said. "I could hear you snoring in there. Maybe you should see a doctor—"

"Shayna, I need you to tell me something. I need you to tell me how old you are."

"I told you, I'm—"

"Nineteen. Maybe in the metric system. What about in years?"

"I don't want to get in trouble."

"Hey, what harm did it do Traci Lords? She's in the movies, right, with her clothes on and everything. I'm not asking you in any official capacity."

"I'm nineteen. I can show you my I.D.—"

"I'm sure you can. Look. Let me ask you something. You say you *like* me—"

"I do. You . . . nothing."

"I remind you of somebody."

"Yes."

"Your old boyfriend."

"No."

Then he knew.

"Your father," he said.

She nodded.

"Did he beat you?"

"No. It was just verbal."

"Did he have . . . relations with you?"

A shrug. "Just once. He knew I was doing it with my boyfriend, so it wasn't like I was a virgin or anything."

There was an interesting rationalization.

"He felt really bad, after," she said. "He even cried."

And now she began to cry again.

"Did you report it?"

Sniffling, she managed, "No."

"You didn't do *anything?*"

"No. Well. I told my mother."

"What did she say, your mother?"

"Nothing. She just . . . nothing."

"What did she say? What did she do?"

"She . . . called me a little slut."

Jesus.

"I'm sorry, Shayna."

"And she slapped me."

"When did you leave?"

"That afternoon. I had some money saved, from my paper route."

"Your paper route?"

Her expression was hurt. "Girls can have paper routes, too, you know."

"Sure they can. Equality being what it is and all. Where are you from?"

"The Midwest."

"See if you can be more specific."

"Brainerd."

"Is there anybody else, there—like an aunt, a sister . . ."

"My aunt's nice."

"Could you live with her?"

"I suppose. She and Mom don't get along that well. At least, they didn't when I was talking to them. It's been six months."

"Did you finish high school?"

"No."

"How were your grades?"

"B's and C's. A's in speech and drama."

"You could go back there. I could help you arrange it, so you could live with your aunt. You could go back and finish."

She was looking at him with a you-must-be-nuts smile. "Why would I want to do that?"

"How old are you?"

Still smiling, she said, "I made a movie. Mr. Giardella says I have star power—"

"How old are you?"

The smile dropped away. Nothing was left but a childishly blank countenance. "Do I have to tell?"

"Yes."

"Fourteen," she said.

He needed company, of the female variety, and since Shayna was a minor, and his ex-wife would rather gargle with drain cleaner than give him a kiss, Sipowicz phoned Lois.

For months now, Lois had been his Tuesday after-shift relief girl. She'd started out as a snitch—like a lot of the higher-class whores in the precinct, she was connected to Giardella—but they'd formed a relationship, Andy and Lois. It was a once-a-week, forty-dollars-a-trick kind of relationship; but a relationship.

He could talk to Lois. She was understanding. She had a friendly ear.

A Saturday session was unusual, but he called her, got her answering machine and left word she could reach him that afternoon at Patrick's, if she had time for some companionship and cared to add a couple of twenty spots to her retirement plan.

He had just knocked back his third bourbon when Lois wandered in. She wore a green dress and a red curly wig; her real hair was mousy, but she had a nice slender face with big brown eyes and looked damn good for thirty-five. Unfortunately, she was twenty-seven.

She slid onto the stool next to him. "Got your message."

"Why didn't you just call me? I'd come to you. I don't expect curb service."

She nodded toward the heavy-set bartender in the Hawaiian shirt; he was giving her the evil eye. "Leon doesn't like to help me do business. Leon doesn't like having me in his establishment at all, to be frank about it."

"You want me to have a little talk with Leon? Leon! Hey, Leon!"

"No, Andy—"

But Sipowicz was bellowing down the bar at Leon. "You want to treat my friends with respect? Or you want me to take my business elsewhere?"

Leon sighed, rolled his eyes, shook his head, and waited on a less contentious client down the bar.

"I put that hump's kid through college," Sipowicz said, and slammed back the fourth of the four shots Leon had lined up for him.

"Forget him, baby," Lois said, touching his arm. "Come let mama take care of you."

Soon they were in her cheap little apartment

around the corner, and he plopped his ass down on the edge of a double bed in a bedroom decorated with a tiger painting and a Holiday Inn abstraction, both of which Lois had picked up at second-hand shops.

"What do you do with your money, anyway?" he asked her. "You haven't invested all that much in interior decorating."

"I put it in the bank," she said, pulling his pants down around his ankles. "I'm saving up."

"Oh, yeah. I forgot. You got family in Florida."

"Orlando," she said, working the pants around his shoes.

"Tourists and old people."

She was unbuttoning his shirt. "Don't be a grouch."

"Do you think I'm an ugly drunk? Some people think I'm an ugly drunk."

She slipped the shirt off him. "I think you're a great big teddy bear."

He clutched her arm. "Don't say that."

"What? Why?"

He let go of her arm. "Nothing. Forget it."

"You're not gonna get physical, are you, Andy? You never got physical before."

"I'm not gonna get physical. Tell me somethin', Lois. Would you ever do porn?"

"No! You think I'm crazy?" She stood and slipped her green dress up over her pale curves, her flesh almost white against the black underwear. She wore black patterned hose—not panty hose, but the garter belt variety, ending halfway up her thighs. For her customers' sake.

He asked, "Why would you not do that?"

She undid her bra. "What if my parents saw it?"

"You think your parents look at garbage like that?"

"I bet my father does. Lay back, now. Let mama do the work. . . ."

Later, Sipowicz—in T-shirt and boxers, on top of the bedspread, a couple pillows propped behind him—smoked and talked to her while she was in the john taking care of business.

"I'm tellin' ya, Lois, that sick wig-wearing sack of shit, he *knew* she was underage. Giardella *helped* her get the fake I.D., but then made her promise she'd never 'tattle' on him."

When she came out of the bathroom, she was back in the green dress again, smoothing it out. "Well, why are you so depressed, Andy? Isn't this what you've been lookin' for? A way to put Alfonse Giardella behind bars?"

"That's the spot I'm in," he said, and sighed. He slid over and sat on the edge of the bed. He was weaving a little—four shots of bourbon's worth—as he bent to pick up his pants.

"Let me help you with those," she said.

Before putting them on, he dug in a pocket. "Is forty enough?"

"It's fifty on Saturday, Andy—but for you, let's keep it friendly and forty." She sat close to him. "It's sweet, you carin' about this kid."

"She's only fourteen."

"She must be pretty cute."

"Why do you say that?"

She grinned slyly at him. "You know. The way you got into it this afternoon."

He flushed. "Don't talk dirty. I think of her like a daughter."

"That never stopped a lot of fathers."

"What do I do, Lois? I'm between a rock and a hard place."

She batted the air, smirked, and said, "Are you kidding? Go for it. Take that bald bastard down. He's no friend of mine."

Sipowicz was nodding. "Kiddie porn—he could go away a long time, if I go that way."

She was looking at him curiously. "What other way to go is there?"

He shrugged. "Help this kid get out of this sleazy life. Help her pack, and put her on a bus, and send her back to America's heartland, if I can locate some relative of hers that loves her but doesn't want to have sex on her."

"Does she *want* to go home?"

Sipowicz grunted a laugh. "She wants to be a movie star."

"Sounds like she already is one."

"I don't know. I don't know. Sendin' Giardella's fat ass away to camp would be so *sweet* . . . but it would be better to get this kid straightened out, don't you think? Better than exposing her to bullshit publicity that'll scar her up for life?"

Lois was nodding, and her half-smile wasn't really

a smile at all. "She'd be a star, all right—on all the tabloid sleaze shows."

"So what do you think, Lois?"

"I think you're very sweet, Andy," she said, and touched his face. "But, hey—I got a four o'clock."

And Sipowicz, his pants on, wandered out of the apartment, down the stairs, and back around the corner to Patrick's, to look for more answers in shot glasses. He didn't find any, of course, but after a while, it didn't matter, because he forgot the questions.

ELEVEN

The drive upstate was pleasant enough, at least after the thruway took them into farm country, where the apple orchards and vineyards of the Wallkill River Valley provided lush late-summer scenic vistas.

But before things got pretty, things got pretty ugly—and it was all Kelly's fault. He knew that. He knew it even as the various patronizing words came tumbling out of his mouth. He tried to stop them— his mind fired off warning shot after warning shot— but the harsh words came out, anyway.

"You go to a private firm," he told Laurie, "they're just gonna take advantage of who and what you know."

She was sitting as close to the passenger's side window as she could, an elbow leaned against the door, hand shading her eyes even though she was wearing sunglasses. The blank eyes of the sunglasses in the reflected glass looked at him, but she didn't.

"All I said was I thinking about it," she said quietly.

"What's the name of this firm, anyway?"

"Did I say some specific firm had made an offer?"

"No. But what firm is it?"

Now she turned to look at him; he was wearing sunglasses, too, but neither his sunglasses nor hers could protect him from her glare.

"I don't suppose there's any chance at all," she said icily, "that some firm might want me for *me*—for my skills, my talents, my qualifications—"

"It's some firm doin' business downtown, isn't it?" Another warning shot fired off in his head but he pressed on. "Sometimes I think you'd do anything to regain your goddamn upward mobility. . . ."

She looked away again. "John . . . don't."

"Must be terrible, bein' weighted down by a civil servant like me. You know what your inside knowledge is worth to those sleazebags, landing somebody right out of the City Attorney's office?"

"That's for me to weigh, isn't it?"

"You're makin' a mistake."

"Then let me make it. I'm a big girl, Johnny. I can take care of myself."

"Can you? If you can't see through slimy overtures like these, I—"

"You're doing it again."

He swallowed. "Doing what again?"

"The overprotective routine."

He watched the road. "No, no. I'm just interested in—"

She turned to look at him and whipped off her sunglasses, all in one motion; her jaw, her whole face, was like stone. "If you want to smother me, Johnny, might I make a suggestion? Do it with a pillow, in my sleep. It'd hurt less."

And he couldn't find anything to say after that, at least not until the scenery kicked in, and he made lame remarks about how great everything looked, the way the sun hit the leaves and all, eliciting nothing from Laurie in response other than an occasional shrug, nod, or grunt as she stayed turned away from him, staring out that window.

Nestled between two mountains, New Paltz was an artsy community, probably due to the state university's art-oriented campus there, its tiny downtown strip littered with New Age–tinged shops. The latter-day hippie feel of the little town was offset by Dutch stone houses dated back to the days of the Huguenots.

The New Paltz Terrace Care Center dated back to another ancient era—the mid-1950s. The lowslung Frank Lloyd Wright-ish brick building sat in cool, slightly sterile serenity on grounds as beautifully manicured as a cemetery.

"You wanna drop me off here awhile?" he asked his wife through the open window on the driver's side; he was out of the car, leaning in. "There's some arts and crafts shops, antiques you could check out."

"Okay," she said, sliding behind the wheel.

"Unless you wanna keep me company."

"I kept you company on the drive," she said crisply. "I'm not going to be your accomplice on your 'mission.' "

"Now *you're* doing it."

"What?"

"I could use some support, here."

"I don't think you should do this." She had her right hand on the wheel, but with her left she touched his hand. "You know, there's some beautiful lodges in the area. We could forget this, and just check in somewhere, and . . . settle our differences."

It was a tempting offer. She hadn't been responsive to him in the bedroom for several days.

"Why don't we do that, after I get done here?" he suggested tentatively, with his patented little-boy smile.

It didn't take.

"I'll pick you up in an hour," she said curtly. "That ought to be time enough for you to spoil some little old lady's weekend."

Then she backed the car out, swung out onto the rest home's drive, and was gone.

He asked at the reception desk if he could visit Helen Watts—Honey Wayne's real name, her married name, according to Norma Moscowitz—and was told he could find her on the sun porch. No questions about whether he was a relative or friend, or if he was expected—people in rest homes apparently weren't particular about who wanted to pay them a visit.

The hallways were wide, the walls brick, the floors a gray mosaic, rather like a school corridor. Paintings of the founders of the home—dignified elderly people themselves—and occasional vases of cut flowers were the primary decorations.

He wandered by a recreation room, its tall tinted windows filtering the sun. The room was filled with old people, some on their feet and chipper, mingling, others in wheelchairs or settled on chairs and couches with walkers at the ready. At four tables, cardplaying was going on; elsewhere, some crocheting, a little reading. Lots of talk, even some laughter.

This was a newer, roomier, cheerier facility than the one where his mother stayed, but the hospital smell was the same, and so was the immediate cloak of depression that wrapped itself around him.

A nurse pointed the way to the curved windows of the sun porch, where two couples had another game of cards going at a table over to the left, and—over by herself—a woman in a wheelchair sat gazing out at the well-tended, flower-brightened grounds.

Her back was to him, but as he angled around to where he could get a look, there was no mistaking her: wrinkles didn't disguise the pretty, heart-shaped face, the big brown eyes, the pert nose, the full mouth. Unlike some older women, particularly ones who had been beautiful, she did not overdo her makeup; just some lipstick, maybe some pancake.

She was heavier—the bosom was still full, only quite a bit lower. A lady in her seventies in a powder-blue pantsuit and a wheelchair, with jeweled reading

glasses on elastic around a creped neck, Helen
Watts—widow of Harold R. Watts, auto parts re-
tailer, mother of two grown daughters and a grown
son—was still very recognizably Honey Wayne.

"Mrs. Watts?"

She'd been lost in thought and his voice startled
her. She turned her head to look at him and smiled
and said, "Yes?"

But then the smile faded and her eyes became
tight in the loose flesh of her face.

"I'll be goddamned," she said, and let out air, as if
she'd been struck a blow; she put a hand to her
chest, breathing hard.

He bent down, putting a hand on the arm of her
wheelchair. "Are you all right, Mrs. Watts?"

She swallowed, took a closer look at him. Still
breathing hard, she nodded. He found a wicker chair
and pulled it near her and sat, leaning in toward her.

"You're sure you're all right?" he asked.

She nodded again. "For a minute I thought you
were someone I . . ." She narrowed the big brown
eyes and studied him. "You, you *must* be . . . you're
his son, aren't you?"

Kelly nodded. "I'm John Kelly, Jr."

She swallowed, composed herself. "You'll have to
forgive me, I . . . you really startled me, is all."

"I'm sorry."

"It's just . . . it's so odd. I was just thinking about
your father . . . and then you spoke, and I turned
. . . well."

"You think about him often?"

She motioned with her right hand. "Sit more in front of me. So I can see you better."

"All right," he said, scooting the wicker chair around.

"I had a stroke two years ago . . . that's why I'm here, a sweet young thing like me. I can't use my left arm and . . . well, anything on my left side from here down."

"I'm sorry."

She bestowed him half a smile. "I appreciate that, young man. But I'm still considered a pretty hot number in these circles. I've got widowers in their eighties lining up to push me around, so to speak."

"I'll bet you do."

She was studying him. "You smile like him. Same little-boy smile—it's the dead giveaway, you know."

"What is?"

"That smile. You're very much like him."

"Look like him, you mean."

"Yes, but that's not what I meant."

"What did you mean?"

"*You're* not as tough as you pretend to be, either."

He laughed a little. "I suppose not. Aren't you wondering why I'm here?"

"I hadn't got that far, really. It's so nice . . . nice to see that freckled face again . . . that red hair. You're . . . you're a cop, too, aren't you?"

"Does it show?"

"You might as well be wearing your badge. Or 'shield,' that's what you call it, isn't it?"

"Is that what my father called it?"

She was studying him again, but not his looks: She was trying to see deeper. "What are you after, John Kelly, Jr.?"

He twitched a smile. "What are cops usually after?"

"An apple off an apple cart. A free doughnut."

"Is that what my father was after?"

"He was a square, your father. That's what made him special. He cared about people. He had a heart where most cops keep their billfolds. What kind of cop are you, John Kelly, Jr.?"

Hunching forward, he clasped his hands in upside-down prayer. "I . . . I thought I was the kind of cop my father was."

"Aren't you sure? Don't you know?"

"Not anymore."

"Why?"

He shrugged. "Because I'm not sure what kind of cop my father was, anymore."

"I see. I see. That's why you're here? You heard things. Rumors."

He nodded.

"Where did you hear these rumors?"

"From a mob guy named Lou Nardi."

She frowned in thought. "Wasn't he just killed?"

"That's right. How did you know?"

She shrugged on her right side. "I watch the news. We have all the latest conveniences here, indoor plumbing, television . . . I didn't hear *your* name on the news. John Kelly, I would have remembered hearing that."

"They do their best to keep the cops' names out, when it's a grand jury detail."

"Even when a witness gets killed?"

He laughed, once. "Especially when a witness gets killed."

Her eyes were tight with thought. "This Lou Nardi—was he part of the Marino family?"

Kelly nodded.

She smiled distantly. "God. It feels funny."

"What does?"

She shook her head. "Even *saying* that name again, after so much time, after all these years—Marino."

"Was Lou Nardi telling the truth, Mrs. Watts?"

"Why don't you call me Helen? That's what your father called me."

"He didn't call you Honey?"

"No. We were friends. He didn't use my stage name."

"I see. Mrs. Watts—Helen—was Lou Nardi telling the truth?"

She smirked at him. "Do you usually give credence to the word of lowlifes?"

"Cops can't always be particular about where they find the truth."

"Mob wiseguy like that wouldn't know the truth if it bit him on the ass." Suddenly she laughed. "If my grandkids could hear me now . . ."

"You have grandkids. That's nice."

"Don't patronize me, John. What did he tell you, this Nardi character?"

"That you killed Tony Marino with an ice pick."

"I see. What else?"

"That my father covered it up."

"I see. Why would your father do that, do you suppose?"

"Because you and he . . ." He couldn't make himself say it.

She nudged him with her words: "What did this Nardi character say?"

"I'd rather not use the language."

"Use it."

"That my father was 'banging' you. Sorry."

She laughed. "You're as square as he was, aren't you?"

"I wouldn't know."

"It's not a bad thing. It's endearing. You're a detective like he was, too. Poking around in things."

"Things that aren't my business?"

"I didn't say it wasn't your business." She raised a finger and shook it gently at him. "But just because things are your business doesn't necessarily make them desirable to know."

"I *have* to know, Mrs. Watts."

"Helen. And why do you have to know, John?"

He enunciated each word individually, evenly: "Because I've built my life on trying to be like him. And if he wasn't the man I *thought* he was, then . . ."

"He was. That and more." She looked at him carefully. "You're not . . . re-opening this investigation, are you?"

"No."

She raised an eyebrow. "Murder cases have no statute of limitations, you know."

"Oh, I know. But I'm not here as a cop."

"How *are* you here, then?"

"As John Kelly's son."

"Have you considered that if you did find out that your father covered up something . . . something *criminal* . . . then not reporting it would make you a sort of accessory . . . way after the fact, but an accessory."

"I don't look at it that way."

"Don't kid yourself: you'd be covering up, too."

She had a point.

"You should walk away, John."

"I can't."

She raised her chin; her expression was pouty—when she was younger, it was an expression that could have gotten most men to give her anything, or do anything for her.

She said, "I don't *have* to tell you."

"Yes, you do," he said, gently.

He stared at her and she stared back at him, until her pouty expression melted into defeat.

She asked him, quietly, "Where shall I start?"

"How did you meet my father?"

"He was interviewing Tony Marino. Trying to tie him to some waterfront killings, union-related. He just about had him, too—till some witnesses died 'accidental' deaths. Your father was hounding Tony, embarrassing him in public, making him stand for frisks, that kind of thing. Anytime there was a crime

with anything at all mob-related attached to it, your
father would come around to Tony's places of business, to the apartment, to the club, and 'question'
Tony."

"What club?"

"I used to work at the Copa. That was something
nice Tony did for me."

"What was?"

"Getting me a job there. It was a classier, show-
business kind of a job. Looking back, though, Tony
was maybe feeling funny about my stripping, and the
cheesecake pictures. Maybe he thought it was better
for his image if I was a showgirl, instead."

"And that's how you met my father."

"Yeah. At the Copa, at the apartment, when he'd
come around, rousting Tony. He'd give me the
'what's a nice girl like you doing with a wrong jerk
like this' routine. Besides, he . . . well, you got to
understand something. Tony started dating me,
'cause . . . well, Tony Marino looked me up for a
very special reason."

Kelly frowned, leaned even closer. "What do you
mean, looked you up?"

"He'd seen me in burlesque. He'd seen me in the
magazines. But most of all, he'd . . . seen me in
those 'special' photos that Norma Moscowitz used to
take of me. The Celebrity News stuff—but you
wouldn't be familiar with that—"

He was nodding. "I know about it."

She cocked her head, finding this hard to believe.
"Little before your time, isn't it?"

"We're talking about bondage photos, aren't we? S and M stuff?"

"That's right, John. Mild by today's standards, but back then—very racy, forbidden, under the counter . . ."

"So Tony . . . he was into that? He was a little kinky that way?"

She rolled her eyes. "More than a little. When we first went out, I thought he was caught up in the glamour thing. You know, I was pretty popular in those magazines. I headlined in burlesque. I even had a couple of bit parts in movies, too—stuff shot in Manhattan; I never went out to Hollywood. Real movies, not loops, no nudity, big-time pictures— there was one with Burt Lancaster where I'm in this low-cut dress sitting at the next table . . . anyway, that's what I thought the attraction was."

"What *was* the attraction?"

Her laugh was humorless. "Let's just put it this way: you cops aren't the only ones into handcuffs. He liked to tie me up, Tony. He liked me helpless. I didn't mind, as long as it didn't get rough, and it didn't get rough, not till he started . . . getting jealous."

"Why did he get jealous, Helen?"

She looked away. "Tony had it in his head I was havin' an affair on him."

"Were you?"

Now she looked right at him, indignant. "What's the difference? Reality was beside the point—in that crazy bastard's head, I was cheating."

"What did he do to you?"

She swallowed. Glanced away. "Bad things."

"Like what?"

"Things . . . with his belt, with cigarettes. I still got scars. I couldn'ta got work with the skin magazines after a couple of *those* sessions, let me tell you. Anyway—your father noticed some burns on my arm and he got me to admit what Tony was doing to me. Your father didn't take that at *all* well—some hood doing a sadistic number on a 'nice kid' like me."

"What did he do about it?"

"He and this partner of his—O'Hara? O'Malley? O'Something. Anyway, this partner of his was rougher than a cob—handsome devil, but tough, man, tough. Older than your dad. Apparently your dad and . . ."

"O'Keefe."

"O'Keefe! That's it! How could I forget? Anyway, he and O'Keefe picked Tony up and walked him down an alley and handcuffed *him* and gave him the worst goddamn beating of his misbegotten life . . . Does that disappoint you, John? That your father would do a thing like that?"

"No."

"Good. Because that son of a bitch Tony deserved it. Trouble was, it didn't really straighten him out. I know your father and his friend wanted to teach Tony a lesson, to scare him into never laying a hand on me again, but guys like Tony Marino, they don't think like normal people."

"He beat you, again."

She nodded. "He beat me so hard and so long, my bruises had bruises. He knocked a tooth out. See this gold one here? He fractured my jaw. My lips were bloody and split. He didn't touch my nose, though—Tony liked my cute little pug nose. And he didn't touch my breasts, either—he didn't want *those* ruined. My entire body was black and blue and purple and brown from bruises except for my titties; they were white like when you're tan everywhere except for your bikini. You should've seen it—it was funny. Really funny. Very damn funny . . ."

"What did you do?"

She shrugged with her right shoulder, and her smile was as tiny as it was strange. "What do you think I did? I waited till he was asleep, and then I took an ice pick and I stabbed Tony Marino thirty-seven times."

Kelly said nothing.

She said, "He woke up after the first blow, but just for a second. That first one was in his chest, but the second was in his throat. Then things got kind of out of hand. I just started flailing at him. He was dead through most of it . . . but I wanted to make sure."

There was laughter from the table where bridge was being played, loud, good-natured arguing.

Kelly asked, quietly, "Then what did you do?"

"I called your father. Do I have to tell you the rest?"

"No."

She stared out at the beautiful lawn, the colorful

flowers. "He blamed himself, your father. He felt that he and his partner, by beating Tony up, had caused the chain of events that led to my going off like that."

"Is that the only reason?"

She turned to look at him. "What other reason would there be, John?"

"Maybe he loved you. Maybe he was having an affair with you, like Tony Marino suspected."

Another right shoulder shrug. "Maybe. Maybe not."

"You're not going to tell me?"

"No."

His smile was amazed, and had little to do with the usual reasons for smiling. "You admit a bloody ice pick murder, and you won't tell me whether you and my father were . . ."

She was placid, self-composed, as she said, "No. I won't tell you. I'll tell you this much: your father was fond of me, and I was fond of him. He wasn't married at the time. . . ."

"But he was dating my mother."

"Yes, he was. But whether he and I were anything more than friends, well, John—that's personal. That's not something you need to know."

"If my father covered up—"

"No 'if.' He did cover up. He covered up a murder I committed. I freely admit that to you. I warned you that if you pressed me, I'd tell you, and you have to live with that."

"I know."

"If you want to get me transferred from this nursing home to a cell, well, that's your call, isn't it?"

"I'm not going to do that."

She returned her gaze to the window, to the lawn. "I never even told my late husband, God rest his soul, in thirty-five years of marriage, what I have just told you. My three kids, they don't know. They think it's kind of fun that their mom used to be a celebrity. Do you know that my magazines are collectible? Norma tells me I'm more popular now than in my heyday, isn't that the damnedest thing? My kids aren't embarrassed about my nudie-cutie days. My son wants me to go on TV and make some money off of it, Whatever Happened to Honey Wayne. Me, I'd rather be remembered the way I used to look. I mean, look at me now, an old lady— look at these poor boobies of mine . . . they've fallen and they can't get up." Her laugh was almost a cackle. "So when my kids ask me questions about those days, I answer them. I'm not ashamed. Not one bit. *But not in that one area, I don't answer any questions.* Kids don't need to get inside their parents' bedrooms. It's personal."

Kelly sat looking at this beautiful old woman, gazing at big brown eyes that were brimming with tears.

And he reached out and squeezed her hand.

"You're right," he said.

He stood.

"I'm sorry to have bothered you, Mrs. Watts."

"You didn't bother me," she said. "How . . . how is your mother?"

The question startled him. "Did you know her?"

"No. But your father spoke of her affectionately. They were engaged when I knew him."

"She's in a place like this, but . . . she's not doing as well as you."

"Oh? I'm sorry to hear that."

"She's not suffering. She . . . she has Alzheimer's."

"Oh, dear."

"Sometimes . . . you know. Sometimes she mistakes me for my father."

Her smile was gentle. "An easy enough mistake to make."

"Good-bye, Mrs. Watts. Helen."

"Don't look so sad. You cheered me up."

"I cheered you up?" He had got her to confess an ice pick murder, he had dredged up a past of bondage and beatings and jealousy, and he had cheered her up?

"It was nice seeing John Kelly again," she said.

He sat on a bench outside, waiting for Laurie. When she pulled up, he got in on the passenger's side.

"Well?"

"Well, she answered some of my questions. Some, she refused to."

"Good for her."

"You don't want to know what we talked about?"

"No. Can we go now?"

"It's two hours home. You up for supper?"

"Well . . . I ran across this place called the Locust Tree Inn. Outdoor dining, trees, old stone house, shallow conversation . . ."

He smiled a little. "You mean, the kind where I don't try to run your life, and you don't try to run mine?"

"Exactly that kind."

"Do they have rooms?"

"Doesn't hurt to ask," she said.

TWELVE

Sipowicz, head throbbing, eyes burning, feeling puffy and bloated, stumbled into the aqua-blue, water stain-ceilinged, paint-peeling, cluttered chamber that was Room 202 at the 15th Precinct. He felt like dogshit under a fat guy's shoe; he felt like a cartoon-character balloon in the Macy's Thanksgiving Day parade about to explode from too much helium. He felt like death warmed over.

In other words, about par for his Monday-morning course, after a cozy Sunday at home with his friends baseball and bourbon, his only other company being his aquarium of saltwater tropicals. At least he hadn't shot a hole in the TV when the ump made that lousy call that would've cost the Mets the game if they weren't already five runs behind.

In his more lucid moments yesterday, he had mulled over the Shayna situation. He had even thought about calling her. Seeing her. But he was afraid of himself. What if his fatherly intentions got away from him, out of weakness of character due to inebriation? What if he landed up in the sack with this fourteen-year-old kid?

Then that would make him as big a slimebucket as Giardella.

Shuddering at the thought, he got himself some coffee in Interview One and wandered back into the bullpen, sat heavily at his desk. John Kelly's jacket was slung over the chair at the desk butted up against Sipowicz's, meaning his partner had beat him to work. Not the first time.

It would be nice having John back. Sipowicz was anxious to get his partner's opinion on whether to give this kid a ticket back to dairyland, or use her to nail Giardella's pasta-fed ass to the wall.

The open window-blinds of the lieutenant's office revealed John in there, having a fairly animated conversation with Fancy. Of course, chunks of granite like the Loo didn't get all that animated; Mickey Mouse he was not. Not even Homer freakin' Simpson . . .

"Detective Sipowicz?"

He turned toward the voice—a woman's voice, well-modulated, businesslike, but feminine. Like its owner, Assistant District Attorney Sylvia Costas.

She was standing on the other side of the rail, near where the receptionist would sit if they had a receptionist. She had short brown hair, a mannish Moe Howard cut offset by a softness of color and stylish combing. Plus, she had a nice full shape on her, unlike some of those skinny yuppie career broads.

But her most striking feature, in an attractive, intelligent face, was her eyes—large, brown, kinder than the almost harsh navy-blue business suit and white blouse she wore, partially offset by the feminine touch of pearl earrings.

"I had a message on my machine that you'd like to speak with me," she said, tentatively. Her expression was guarded, and a little suspicious.

His reputation had preceded him.

He stood and gestured for her to come through the gate. "I left word for you over the weekend," he said. "I didn't mean you should make a special trip. I knew you had that burglary case that Roberts brought in, and . . ."

She walked over and planted herself firmly on two feet, weight equally displaced, and held her briefcase like a huge fig leaf before her as she stood looking down at him.

"I didn't make a special trip, Detective. But I have a minute to spare."

A minute! Wasn't that generous of her? Who did this woman think she was, anyway?

"Look," he said, trying not to sound defensive, and failing, "I got a situation and I need a legal reading on it."

She raised an eyebrow. "All right."

"I got a possible child pornography pop that I'm

worried if I should bring it in, it could ruin the life of the child in question . . ."

She moved her head to one side, squinting at him; it was a cautionary expression, as were her words: "Detective, do I have to remind you that as an officer of the court, if I have knowledge of a crime, I have to—"

Sipowicz smiled as he loosened his collar with an inserted finger. "Uh, Ms. Costas, I think you weren't listening that carefully. You may not have heard where I said this was a hypothetical situation."

She nodded, the big brown eyes half-lidded; he had taken her prompt.

"Anyway," he continued, "hypothetically, I could put Alfonse Giardella away on this charge."

Her eyes came alive at the sound of Giardella's name.

Sipowicz went on. "There's a stripper in one of his clubs, fourteen, she's done a porno for him."

"Did she show him false I.D.? That would make it tougher—not impossible, but—"

"She didn't show him false I.D. The prick *provided* her false I.D. He knowingly put a fourteen-year-old in front of a dick and a camera."

"Would she make a good witness?"

"Very credible girl. Nice girl. Good student."

She raised an eyebrow again. "She just happens to strip and make porno films."

"One porno film, and I don't really think you should be judging some poor kid who didn't have the world handed to her on no freakin' silver spoon. She missed out on the Vassar scholarship, if you catch my drift."

She was looking down at him again. "I catch your drift, Detective. What's your question? It sounds like a makeable case."

"Oh, it's makeable, all right. I just wonder—is it worth it? What it would put this kid through?"

"That's not a legal question, Detective. It's more a value judgment. A moral and ethical decision. Not that I'm not pleasantly surprised that you might be concerned about such matters."

"Hey, stick around, Ms. Costas. I'm full of surprises. I'm a human Cracker Jack box. Can you hypothetically help me on this, or not?"

"You're wondering if I could help keep the girl's name out of the papers? Keep this low-profile?"

"That's what I'm wondering."

She thought about it, and her mouth was a thin, regretful line. "I couldn't promise you. With a high-profile defendant like Alfonse Giardella, the media is going to be ants at a picnic. And, of course, the girl would be in a certain amount of danger—although we could provide police protection . . . though as I'm sure you're aware, there *have* been instances where police protection didn't insure the safety of sequestered witnesses . . . if you catch my drift, Detective?"

He smirked at her. "I caught it a long time ago, Ms. Costas. But it's okay—I had my shots."

She sighed, shrugged. "I could lie to you—but that's the truth of it."

"Well . . . I appreciate that much."

"You're welcome." Her face tightened into a momentary smile. "Good luck with your moral dilemma, Detective Sipowicz."

He watched her go. He bet there was a nice body lurking under that business suit—not that he figured he'd ever find out. Somehow he had a hunch that he wasn't this broad's type.

Turning toward the windows of the lieutenant's office, Sipowicz was surprised to see John still going at it with Fancy in there; not bad for a guy with his arm in a sling.

Sipowicz knew he and Fancy had what you might call a strained relationship; whereas his partner, John, got along famously with the lieutenant.

So when John stormed out of the Loo's office, his Irish mug as red as a pimple about to pop, Sipowicz took notice.

"Shit," John said, sitting down hard.

"You and Mount Rushmore have a little spat?"

"I'm off the street. It's policy, he says. You're out wounded a week, when you come back, it's a minimum of ten days ass duty."

Sipowicz frowned. "I figured you'd jump in with me, on this Giardella/Viana thing . . ."

"No. You and that kid from Anti-Crime stay on it. Me, I'll be takin' crank calls, handling the community policing logs, filing stop-and-frisk reports . . ."

"Police work," Sipowicz said. "Not just a career, but a job."

The lieutenant was standing in his office, looking through the slats of the window blinds at them. For a man whose facial expressions ran the gamut from absent to zero, Fancy could convey a world of disapproval with a glance.

And this was a stare.

"I'm gonna take a piss," Sipowicz said, scooting his chair back and standing. "When the Loo stops shootin' laser beams in this direction, why don't you find an excuse to join me?"

A few minutes later, Sipowicz was sneaking a smoke in the locker room just beyond the bullpen. The white-tile and green-plaster glorified cubicle, with its coverless toilet seats, low-flying mirror over a couple pitiful sinks, and curtained single shower stall, also served as the squad's unisex toilet. For this reason, the doors could be locked behind you—which John did.

"This may not be about you," Sipowicz said, tossing his cigarette butt into the nearest crapper; he kicked the flush handle. "I think maybe it's about me."

"What do you mean?"

"I mean, I think maybe the lieutenant wants to phase out our partnership."

"Why would he do that?"

"He likes you. He sees a future for you. Bein' stuck with a loser like yours truly isn't exactly a blueprint for gettin' ahead in the department."

"I don't look at it that way, and anyway, I don't care."

"I think Fancy does . . . and maybe he's got a point."

"Bullshit."

Sipowicz shrugged, went to the sink, ran water, splashed some up on his puffy face, kept up eye contact with his partner in the mirror. "Well . . . maybe on this case, he does. He's cut me a surprising amount of slack on this one, John. He wants Giardella brought down, just like we do, and he knows how far I'm liable to go."

John frowned in thought.

"He's willing to risk me and my career," Sipowicz said, drying his face with a paper towel. "What's to risk? But, you—he doesn't want you brought down with me, if it comes to that."

"Jesus, Andy—*I'm* the one that got shot."

Sipowicz felt the blood leave his face; shame rushed through him like negative adrenaline. "I think I got a pretty good grasp of that fact. Look, kid—much as I'd like to have you in on this with me, maybe the Loo's right. Keep your distance, for a week or ten days."

John was shaking his head, no—almost violently. "This is *my* case, too."

Sipowicz touched his partner's arm. "I know it is. I know it is. I'll bring you in at the finish, Fancy be damned. Okay? Is that a deal?"

John sucked in air, held, then released it and nodded. "I can live with that."

"Listen—you okay at home?"

"Yeah. I'm fine."

"I mean, that's why you really stayed home, right? Spend some time with the little woman?"

"We're doin' all right."

"I mean, I'm not exactly a licensed marital counselor, but I do have some miles on this track."

"I know. It's fine."

"Okay." Sipowicz sighed. "In the meantime, I got a 'moral dilemma.'"

Hearing those words from Sipowicz seemed to amuse John. "What . . . ?"

"I could use your input. You bein' so much more sensitive than a horse's ass like me."

And he filled John in on the Shayna situation.

"It's a tough call," John said, shaking his head.

"What would you do?"

"I don't want to make your mind up for you."

"What would you do?"

"I know how much you want Giardella's ass nailed to the wall."

"What would you *do*?"

"I wanna see that bastard set up housekeeping at Sing Sing as bad as you, Andy—"

"Dammit, John, what would you do?"

He shrugged. "Put the girl on a bus."

Back out in the bullpen, at his desk, Sipowicz took a look at his bank book; he was a little ahead, now that his son was old enough that child support payments had stopped. He figured he could let the girl have five hundred, easy. It wasn't like she was a doper—she could be trusted with the money, though he figured he'd literally help her pack and escort her to the bus station, buy her the one-way ticket, and pat her sweet little behind good-bye.

He was just picturing the girl's face framed in the bus window, waving farewell to her Good Samaritan, when the phone rang.

"Andy . . . it's Lois."

"You know, it's not really a good idea calling me here."

"Patrick's in five minutes."

"Lois, I'm workin' here."

"This *is* work. I can't tell you this over the phone. If you don't see what I look like, you'll kill me."

"Kill you? What . . . ?"

"Five minutes, Andy."

He was there in four. The bar had just opened, at nine, and was doing almost no business. Leon, in his aloha shirt, was wiping glasses.

"Little early for you, ain't it?" the bartender asked.

"Don't set me up anything," Sipowicz said, sweating. He was sticking to his four o'clock rule if it killed him. He took a back booth and for the two and a half minutes it took Lois to get there, Sipowicz stared at the bottles behind the bar like an ancient sailor trying not to get lured toward the rocks by a siren's song.

Lois had on a ratty blond wig with a scarf tied over it, and sunglasses so big her face was an afterthought behind them. She wore a baggy old I ♡ NEW YORK T-shirt, worn-out jeans, and shabby sneakers, and couldn't have looked less like a woman you would pay for sex.

She slid into the booth across from him. She swallowed hard. "Don't kill me."

"What's this 'kill you' crap?"

She gingerly removed the sunglasses; both her eyes were black and swollen—the left one was, in fact, swollen shut.

Rage boiled through him. "Who did this to you?"

"Giardella."

"That fat fuck! *Why?*"

"I wouldn't tell him."

"Tell him what, Lois?"

"What you told me."

"What I told you. What did I tell you?"

"That's what he wanted to know."

"This is startin' to sound like who's on freakin' first. Why did he beat you up, Lois? What did he want to know?"

She put the glasses back on; she seemed to be trying to disappear within herself, or the booth, at least. "He knows you're a regular trick of mine."

Sipowicz shrugged, looking toward the bottles. "It's no secret."

"He thought maybe you spilled somethin' besides what you usually spill."

"I try to be discreet."

She leaned forward. "But you weren't, Andy—you told me about that girl—"

He lashed out and gripped her wrist. "What did you tell him, Lois?"

"Don't hurt me. Don't kill me."

"What. Did. You. Tell. Him."

"Nothing, at first. I told him you never tell me anything about your work . . . but it's not true. You do talk to me, about all kinds of stuff, and I'm a lousy liar, Andy. He could tell I was lying, and he beat me till I told him."

"Told him what?"

"You're hurting me!"

He let go of her wrist. "Told him what?"

"What you told me about the girl."

He didn't remember. He'd been half in the bag when he'd had that Saturday rendezvous with Lois. *What had he told her?*

"I told him," she said, "that you knew this girl he used in triple-X was underage."

"I should kill you," he said, already half out the booth.

"I didn't have to tell you," she said. "If Giardella finds out I told you, *he'll* kill me."

"I won't tell him," Sipowicz said bitterly. "I'll be discreet."

But Lois didn't hear the last sentence, because Sipowicz was halfway out the bar.

He took time to go back to the station house, up to the squadroom, to collect John.

"Come on," he said.

John looked up from paperwork and said, "Where?"

"No questions."

"You're supposed to work with Martinez."

"He's testifying on some Anti-Crime case. You available to fill in?"

John was looking at the lieutenant's office, where Fancy was on the phone.

"Sure," he said, leaving his sling behind, following the already exiting Sipowicz.

The apartment door was locked, and there was no answer to Sipowicz's knocking as it echoed down the crummy hallway.

"Way too early for her to be at work," Sipowicz said darkly.

"She could be out shopping," John offered.

"Let's get the super."

The super was tall, skinny, sunken-eyed, with long stringy hair and a stubbly beard; he could have been a dope addict, but he was just an artist who looked after the building in exchange for the apartment he used as his studio. His smock was smeared with paint, and so were his jeans; his feet were in sandals. He looked like a cross between Jesus Christ and Maynard G. Krebs.

"Aren't you supposed to have a warrant or something?" he asked, as he led them down the hallway back to the girl's apartment. His voice was masculine and bassy, but his tone and diction had a timidity about them.

"I thought I heard a cry for help in there," Sipowicz said.

"That's what we call probable cause," John said.

"Now open the door with your master key," Sipowicz said, "before I use your goddamn head for a battering ram."

The super opened the door and backed away. There was something about the way he did it, something about his manner, that gnawed at Sipowicz's gut.

But there was no time for reflection. He moved quickly through the little living room, with its TV and VCR and all those tapes of those Hollywood movies Shayna loved so much, and they found her in the hot pink bedroom, in the chipped-veneer '40s deco bed, under the sheet, among her teddy bears, pop stars, and movie idols staring down at her from posters.

She'd been shot in the chest, twice, right through the sheet; either she'd been sleeping on her back, or turned that way when her would-be killer came in.

Would-be.

She was still alive. Sipowicz found a pulse in the cold wrist of the cold arm, even though the bed was shades of scarlet and brown from the blood she'd lost. The mattress was blood-soaked; so were the undersides of the teddy bears. She'd been shot long enough ago that some of this blood was dried; it was a miracle she was still alive.

John was out in the other room, calling 911, calling for the Mobile Crime Scene Unit, while Sipowicz stroked the cold forehead, begging the child not to die.

THIRTEEN

Kelly and Andy snapped on rubber gloves and had a last look around the girl's apartment, before turning it over to the Crime Scene Unit, waiting in the wings.

"Nine millimeter," Kelly said, crouching, holding a shell casing between thumb and middle finger.

"That's Viana's utensil of choice, you know," Andy said, milling restlessly around the little bedroom, eyes flicking from this pop-star poster face to that one, as if hoping these silent witnesses to the crime would suddenly start talking.

Kelly, putting two nine-millimeter shells in an evidence envelope, stood. "You really think Viana's still around? He's had plenty of time to skip, and there hasn't been a trace of him in a week."

Andy shrugged. "Just a feeling I got."

Kelly shrugged with his eyebrows. "Well, this

went down before dawn, and nobody's copping to hearing any gunshots."

Once the girl was in the ambulance and on her way to Roosevelt Hospital, with a uniformed man holding the apartment for the Crime Scene Unit, Kelly and Andy had done a brief canvass of the other tenants. A few were at work, but enough were on hand—college kids, mostly—to believably confirm nobody had heard shots or seen anybody suspicious.

"Viana and Persico," Andy said, "when they threw that little surprise party at the Hotel Savory, used noise-suppressed nine millimeters."

Kelly nodded. "And we got no forcible entry."

"I figure the kid was asleep when she was shot."

"So somebody walked right in."

Andy glanced out toward the living room. "Yeah. It's almost like they had a key."

"How's that super look to you?"

"Like he's carryin' a heavy burden he wants to unload."

"Wanna go talk to him?"

Andy nodded; his mouth twitched. "Yeah—but not in his 'artist's studio.' Let's bring him down here—let's talk to him right here in this bedroom, where he can enjoy that abstract painting in blood there."

Kelly was shaking his head in doubt. "I wouldn't want anybody accusing us of compromising this crime scene . . ."

"Now there's a hell of an idea." Andy's smile was horrible. "You got an extra pair of rubber gloves?"

Soon Andy was ushering the hippie-haired, sunken-eyed landlord, whose name was Victor Hagenwalter, past the uniformed cop at the door and into the living room. The startled, Manson-esque, string-bean building superintendent nervously tugged on the rubber gloves Kelly had provided him.

"See, Mr. Hagenwalter," Andy was saying, "it's our policy to bring in whoever's responsible for the building, you know, to see if there's anything unusual about the crime scene. Anything out of order."

Kelly asked matter-of-factly, "How well did you know the victim, Mr. Hagenwalter?"

"Not well," he said. The bassy register of his voice just didn't fit its timid tremor. "We used to say hello in the hall sometimes."

Andy's smile might have been friendly. "Really? But you were in her apartment, from time to time, doin' your routine building maintenance, and the like."

"Of course."

Kelly gestured around the living room. "So, does anything seem out of place, here? Anything missing?"

"Nothing comes to mind," he said.

Andy smiled and gestured toward the doorless doorway of the bedroom. "Why don't we step in here, Mr. Hagenwalter?"

"I, uh . . . don't remember ever being in her bedroom."

"Come on—you never looked at the heat register in there or anything? Take a look anyway." Andy

took him by the skinny arm and eased him in.
"Maybe something will come to you."

The sunken eyes widened at the sight of the blood-
splotched sheet and mattress. "Oh, Jesus . . . can I
please go now?"

"You're free to go at any time," Andy said. "She's
a nice kid, Shayna."

"Yes."

"Touch and go. She may not make it."

"That's awful."

"Who'd you let in here last night, Victor?"

"What?"

"Who'd you give your passkey to?"

"I didn't give my passkey to anybody!"

"How'd he get in, then?"

"Maybe *she* let him in . . ."

"She was shot in her sleep, Victor."

"Maybe he had a key, maybe he was a boyfriend."

"*Did* she have a boyfriend, Victor?"

"Not really."

"Somebody she was seeing regularly?"

"No."

"You seem pretty sure this was a man, Victor. You
keep saying 'he' did this, she let 'him' in, maybe . . .
so tell us about this man you saw."

"I didn't see anybody . . . I was just assuming it
was a—"

Kelly said, "You know, Victor, this could be something very innocent, or it could be something serious.
The kind of serious you go away for."

"What do you mean?"

"Kelly shrugged, twitched a frown. "Well, if this girl dies, and somebody knowingly let the killer in, well that somebody could be viewed as an accomplice."

"Accomplice . . ."

"First-degree murder, Victor," Andy said. "You and the shooter, you win the same big prize. Dinner of your choice and seats for two, courtesy of Con Ed."

Hagenwalter swung his gaze from cop to cop, his stringy hair swinging; perhaps he was trying to figure out which of them was the "good cop," and which the "bad."

"Do I need an attorney?" he asked Kelly.

Kelly answered with more questions: "Do you, Victor? Did you do something wrong?"

"No, I—"

"I'm gonna guess something, Victor," Andy said. "I'm gonna guess this building, here, this plush condominium high-rise you look after, is owned by a corporation."

"Well . . . Yes . . ."

"And I'm also gonna guess that at the top of that corporate food chain is a gentleman who's a little on the obese side of the spectrum and who wears a wig that matches an outstanding description we have of a missing Venezuelan swamp rat."

The eyes in the deep sockets were narrow and desperate and darting now. "I didn't do anything wrong . . ."

"A girl got shot here, Victor," Kelly said. "Maybe

killed. Now we didn't mention the name Giardella—"

"Please . . . I could get killed . . ."

"Really?" Andy asked. "Why is that?"

He held up his hands in a stop motion. "I'm going now."

"That's fine. But let me tell you *where* you're going: the Fifteenth Precinct station house. You want to grab your beret or your paintbrushes or anything, Victor? You might be awhile."

"It doesn't have to be this way, Victor," Kelly said.

"It doesn't?"

"No. No. You could have been an innocent victim of circumstance . . ."

"You know," Andy said bitterly, "like the Three Stooges?"

"Maybe somebody called you," Kelly said, "representing the ownership of this building, and asked you to give somebody a key. Somebody who just stopped by. Somebody you didn't even know. Somebody you had no idea was going to use that key to open a door and commit this terrible crime."

"What if I just put the key under the mat," he said. "And didn't even see the guy."

Andy sighed heavily. "Then we would have a problem, Victor. Because what we're looking for, to magically transform you from an accomplice into an innocent bystander, not to mention a good citizen with the public's best interests at heart, is a description of the guy you gave the key to."

"If you didn't get a look at him," Kelly said, "then

we're gonna take you down to the station house and treat you like a suspect."

"And then maybe we'll spring you after a while," Andy said with a nasty smile, "only spread the word you rolled over and spread wide, where Giardella was concerned."

His jaw dropped. "You wouldn't do that! You'd be sentencing me to death!"

Andy grabbed the guy by the front of his grungy smock and hauled him over to the bed and pushed his face a quarter of an inch away from the blood-soaked sheet—a place where it was still wet. Where the smell of blood still rose like an awful perfume.

"Did I fail to mention, Victor," Andy said through clenched teeth, "that this girl Shayna is a personal friend of mine? That I would be eternally grateful if you would help us out, here? Or would you rather I shove your face into her blood and moosh it around a little? What do they call that, Expressionism, or is it Impressionism? I forget."

"If I help," he whimpered, "it ends there?"

"I can't guarantee that, Victor."

Kelly, who was watching this, arms folded, as placid and detachedly interested as if watching a ballet, said, "We can guarantee you'll be viewed as a friendly witness, Victor—there will be no 'accomplice' talk."

Andy was still holding the guy's face over the bloody bed.

"I'll help," Hagenwalter said.

Andy hauled him back on his feet and said, "You

mind coming over with us, Mr. Hagenwalter, and looking at some pictures?"

Hagenwalter frowned in thought. "I don't think I need to."

"What's that supposed to mean?"

Hagenwalter took a breath, thought for a moment, then said, "If I could send you in the right direction, could we skip that step?"

Kelly asked, "Do you know who did this?"

He shook his head no, and the hair swung again in greasy arcs. "And I wasn't lying about putting the key under the mat, either, but . . . damnit to hell, I was curious. I peeked at the guy in the hallway."

"Did he see you?" Andy asked.

"No."

"You're sure of that?"

"I'm sure."

Confused, Kelly asked, "So if you never saw him before, how can you I.D. him without a picture?"

"Actually," Hagenwalter said, "I can I.D. him *with* a picture. Come to my studio for a second."

The lanky super led them to his apartment and said, "This won't take long."

Andy grabbed a spindly arm. "You're not thinkin' of retirin' to Florida by way of a fire escape, are you?"

"No, no!"

"Because you'd suddenly be an accomplice again. A potentially dead accomplice."

"I said I'd help!"

And he ducked inside his apartment. Andy was flinching and casting his gaze around even more

nervously than ever; Kelly just leaned against the
wall, hands in pants pockets, patiently waiting.

In under four minutes, Hagenwalter returned. He
had a sheet of sketchpad paper in his grasp.

"I work abstract," Hagenwalter said, "but like
all good abstract practitioners, I have a grounding
in realism."

And he held up a pencil sketch of a shovel-jawed,
five-o'clock–shadowed white male with heavy black
eyebrows over small dead eyes.

Andy snatched the sheet out of Hagenwalter's
hand and stared at the image. Kelly was looking at it,
too, head cocked, his mouth twisted in a humorless
smirk.

"Looks like as of early this morning, anyway,"
Kelly said, "Sal Viana was still in town."

Back at the station house, Kelly was surprised to
find Fancy forgiving about his leaving his desk to
help Andy out. The lieutenant seemed more focused
on Sal Viana.

Looking up from his desk at the two detectives,
Fancy said, "We've got rhythm with Port Authority
P.D., monitoring all bus, rail, and air terminals."

"Good," Andy said. "Maybe after this second kill,
Viana finally *will* take off for parts unknown."

"Any other ideas, gentlemen?" Fancy asked. "You
think another run at the suspect's Canarsie haunts
would do any good?"

"I think," Andy said, "we should grab one of

Giardella's front bumpers and shake him till either his organs or some information falls out."

"Well," Fancy said evenly, "that would certainly not be something I would condone."

"Yeah," Andy said, "like Nixon said, 'That would be wrong.' "

Fancy looked over at Kelly. Then he shifted his gaze to Andy. "A word with you, Detective. Alone."

"We're partners, Lieutenant," Kelly offered defensively.

"Any Dodge City action," Andy said quietly, "is not gonna involve John. Is that what you want to hear, Lieutenant? I'm content destroying one career."

Fancy sighed, again looked from Kelly's face to Andy's, sighed heavily, saying, "Go."

Soon they were at their desks and Andy was rubbing his face with both hands. Then he began to rise. "Cover for me—I'm gonna go over to Roosevelt, see how the girl is doin'."

Kelly looked up skeptically. "You're not thinkin' about goin' over to Minetta's Restaurant and making that dream of yours come true, regarding one of Giardella's front bumpers?"

"No. I'm gonna see how the girl is doin'. Okay?"

"I understand you had to say what you had to say to Fancy. Otherwise he would glue my ass to this chair at this desk. But we're in this Giardella thing together, Andy."

"John, you got my word—"

"Detective!"

It was that kid from Anti-Crime, sauntering in. He had an inoffensively cocky way about him; a blue tie was attached to an explosion-of-colors shirt. He was holding out a slip of paper.

"I see from your formal attire, Martinez," Andy said dryly, "you been in court."

"Yeah, piece a cake," he said with a contagious grin. He pushed through the gate, handing the paper toward Andy.

"Officer Licalsi asked me to bring this up," Martinez said. "Some woman walked in, about fifteen minutes ago. Since you weren't here, she left this message with the Sarge."

"Who's Officer Licalsi?" Kelly asked.

"New blood," Andy said, looking at the slip of paper. "Transferred over from the One-Six in Queens."

"Nice-looking lady," Martinez said, then shrugged, smiled, and—with Kelly at the desk next to Andy—headed back upstairs to Anti-Crime.

Andy grimaced as he wadded up the note and tossed it in his basket. Then, too casually, he said to Kelly, "You up for Patrick's?"

Kelly felt like frowning, but he smiled. "Why? You buyin'?"

"I'm not even drinkin'." Andy pushed up from his desk to his feet. "But I got a feeling it's gonna be real refreshing just the same."

Andy's prostitute, Lois, was in the back booth, wearing a scarf-wrapped blond wig, big sunglasses, and a T-shirt. She was smoking, and was so nervous, it made Andy look calm.

Kelly got in across from the woman, and Andy got in on her side of the booth. She slipped off the sunglasses, revealing twin shiners, and gestured with the glasses toward Kelly—but spoke to Andy.

"I don't wanna talk in front of *him*," she said.

"You say what you gotta say, and say it now," Andy said coldly. He reached out and took her wrist and held it firmly in his hand. "Right now."

She swallowed, and her fake lashes fluttered as she said, "Giardella came around. He does that sometimes."

"Thanks for sharing," he said. "Get to the pertinent part."

"It wasn't sex," she said.

"Get to it, Lois."

"He wanted to thank me for . . . you know. The information. Gave me some cash. Said he didn't like havin' to hurt me. Anyway, while he was talking to me, his beeper went off."

Kelly had to laugh; hoods with beepers. What a great wide wonderful world of technology it was.

"He asked me to use my phone," she said. "I said sure. He called somebody named Sal."

Kelly leaned forward. Andy leaned in, too, to where his head was almost touching hers.

She went on: "He told this Sal to take a room at the Howard Johnson's in midtown. Said he'd have transportation arranged by six o'clock."

"When was this?"

"This morning."

Andy's mouth twitched; his eyes congealed. "Why you'd take so long to tell me, Lois?"

"I was scared. I had to think about it. I came through, didn't I? I wanted to . . . wanted to make it up to you. Isn't this who you're lookin' for, Andy? This Sal something?"

"How do you know that?"

She shrugged. "You told me Saturday afternoon."

"Lois, do me a favor," Andy said sheepishly. "Next time I start spilling my guts to you, stick a tit in my mouth or something."

She shrugged. "Whatever you say, Andy. Let me outta here, would ya? This is too goddamn dangerous, okay?"

"No," Kelly said, sliding out. "We'll go first."

"We're in more of a hurry than you are," Andy said, but he was already out of the booth, moving toward the door.

In the car, Kelly—riding—said, "You really think we need the siren? It's not even close to six."

"I'm anxious, all right?"

"We should call this in. We should go in by the book and with backup. The lieutenant is not going to like this."

Andy gestured with an open palm, his other hand on the wheel. "What have we got to go on? It's just a lead from my 'round-the-world girl, right? Just something we're chasin' down 'cause snitches aren't to be ignored."

"And if it's solid," Kelly said, "we call for back-up?"

"Yeah. Probably."

The Howard Johnson in midtown was between West 51st and 52nd. Andy—who had cut the siren two blocks away—pulled into the motel garage, showed the attendant his badge, and parked.

As Andy got out, he said, "Look, John—we call this in, we gotta involve Midtown North. Then it isn't even our case anymore."

Kelly came around the parked sedan and put his hand on his fidgety partner's shoulder. "Let's just think this through, now. Isn't this all a little too convenient?"

"What?"

"You been lookin' for Viana for a week, then he pulls a second hit, and suddenly Giardella accidentally lets your snitch overhear where Sal is staying?"

"Hey, dumb shit happens. You think this is, what? A trap? Yeah, maybe you're right. We go through the door, somebody's dug a big hole and filled it with alligators."

"That's what you're up to your ass in, my friend," Kelly said. "You know why Giardella wanted you to catch this tip?"

"No. Enlighten me."

Kelly thumped his partner's chest with a forefinger. "Because he knows you'll go through Viana's door blasting. He knows you're a hotheaded hump, and he's banking on you to tie up this loose end for him."

"That's what you think, is it?"

"Yeah. Yeah. That's exactly what I think."

Sipowicz did a Dangerfield neck twist. "You know what I think?"

"What do you think?"

"I think you're right."

"So." Kelly gestured with two hands; his shoulder didn't hurt much anymore. "What do we do about it? Who do you want? The trigger, or Giardella, who squeezed it?"

Andy shrugged, smiled a little. "Why don't we, since we're in the neighborhood and all, go take this prick Viana into custody. Alive and in pristine freakin' condition."

Kelly smiled, squeezed his partner's shoulder. "I wonder what kind of voice Viana has? Somehow I just know he's gonna sing real pretty."

They got the body armor vests and blue NYC POLICE windbreakers out of the trunk and put them on, catching a few concerned glances as they moved into the lobby.

At the desk, the pretty Hispanic clerk recognized the super's sketch of Viana instantly; it was Mr. Smith in room 209—a corner room.

"Is it a suite or anything?" Andy asked.

"No," she said. "Just one large room and a bath."

"How's the room laid out exactly?"

"I can show you our brochure."

"Would you do that? That would be nice."

Kelly asked, "He is alone?"

She was plucking a brochure from a small display rack. "Far as I know."

Andy took the brochure, thanked her, and said, "We'll need the key. You do have a spare?"

"Yes, but, uh . . . you're supposed to have some kind of court order thing, before I'm allowed to do that."

"We had an anonymous tip," Andy said, "that there were sounds of abusive behavior comin' from that room. It's critical we act quickly. You know, time it takes to find a judge, some poor woman can have a fractured skull."

"Oh, dear," she said.

Kelly smiled pleasantly, held an open palm out to her. "We call it probable cause."

And she filled Kelly's hand with the spare card key to room 209.

They took the elevator up to the second floor. The bed, a king size, would be immediately opposite the door as they came in. That was a break; a lot of motel rooms had a kind of hallway with the bed off around the bathroom, at a jog.

But this should be, to quote the kid from Anti-Crime, a piece a cake.

Kelly unlocked the door with the card and shouldered it open, popping the night latch, as Andy burst past him inside the room, .38 thrust before him in a two-handed grasp.

"Police!" Andy yelled. "Let me see your hands!"

Kelly followed, .38 in one hand, shield held outright in the other, and there he was, Salvatore

Viana—a broad-shouldered blue-bearded bruiser caught with his pants literally down (they were visible draped over a nearby chair), those mustache-like eyebrows raised in surprise as he lay in bed, on his back, under a sheet, his chest bare, his pock-marked face a blank mask that quickly twisted into rage.

Everything about the layout of the room was exactly as the pretty desk clerk had told them—only one piece of her information had been inaccurate, or incomplete, anyway.

Viana was not alone.

There were, under the sheet, two women with him—"girls" would be a better description, as it was unlikely they'd seen twenty. A black one was at the left, between Viana and the nightstand where the suppressed nine millimeter lay among his watch, cigarettes, change, and other more innocent possessions, and a big-haired blonde at right, with fake tits and a skinny junkie's frame.

"Hands!" Kelly yelled, as he and Andy fanned out before the bed, having taken in the entire tableau in a millisecond.

But Viana didn't put his hands in the air. He put them on the black girl, a naturally busty, pug-nosed chocolate confection wearing nothing but hair, who squealed in fear as she found herself between Viana and the guns of the police facing them.

And Viana, using the black girl to shield him, snatched the nine millimeter from the bedstand and pointed it around at the two cops.

"It's not gonna work, dickhead!" Andy advised him.

But Viana was not stupid. He reached out and grabbed the other girl as well, and—still in bed—had them both hugged to him, the gun-in-hand peeking around the black girl, his other hand roughly clutching the belly of the blond junkie, who was whimpering.

And then there was a terrible moment of stalemate.

"Here's how it's gonna be," Viana said finally, his voice a breathy cigarette-ruined thing, "I'm using these bitches as *my* body armor, *capeesh*? And the beauty part is, I can lose one of them and still have a hostage."

"It's not gonna work," Andy said quietly.

Viana, in Jockey shorts, was sliding out of bed, taking the girls with him—the black one squealing, the blonde whimpering, kicking a little—onto the floor, all three of them on their feet now. Kelly looked for a clean shot around the wall of human flesh, but there wasn't one.

From where Andy stood, a head shot might be possible.

Kelly said, "Sal, this isn't wise. We got you all jammed up. Backup you'll never wade through. Snipers. SWAT. The whole nine yards."

A flash of smile in the sea of pockmarks and blue stubble. "I got my girls, here, to keep me warm."

Andy said, "You think the mayor's gonna give a

pus-pimple like you a jet to South America or something? Get real."

Kelly said, "You can still come out of this smellin'
like a rose, Sal."

From behind his hostages, Viana barely peeked
out, the silencer-nosed automatic pointing at them.
"Explain how *that* fairy tale comes true," he said in
that grotesque breathy voice.

"Giardella gave you up," Kelly said. "He tipped us.
He expected Andy here to blow your brains out, or
maybe me—after all, you did shoot me."

"You're a lucky man," Viana said. "Most people
don't walk away from what I do."

"You can walk away, Sal," Kelly said, his voice
calm, the gun in his hand taut. "Right into the
Witness Protection Program. I can picture you in a
split-level in Phoenix."

Viana's head bobbed into view and revealed a
sneer. "If you think I buy Giardella dropping the
dime—"

"So how'd we happen upon room 209, here, Sal?"
Andy interrupted. "The Psychic Hotline?"

Edging around from beside the black girl's head,
Viana peered, eyes flickering. "Make your pitch."

"Roll over on Giardella," Kelly said. "It'll go easy
on you."

"Let's all give the orgy girls a free pass," Andy
said, "and go have some roast hog with a side of wig
for supper."

"I don't rat," Viana said.

"You were ratted on," Kelly said.

"No," Viana said, all but disappearing behind his female wall. "I got a free pass out of here. In fact, I got two free passes. Like I said, I can blow one's brains out, and still have a shield. I could maneuver better with one, anyway."

"Do that and you're dead, Sal," Andy said.

"I don't think so. You want *both* these bitches on your head?"

The blonde was whimpering; the black girl's squealing had turned into deep, choking sobs.

"I think you need a demonstration," Viana said, and he put the nine millimeter to the black girl's temple and his finger was squeezing when the sound of a gunshot shook the room, and shook Sal, too, as the right side of his skull went flying off, careening off the wall like a banking billiards shot, and bloody brain matter splattered onto a framed print of a sailing ship, then slid slowly down.

Gun in hand, Sal Viana fell against the nightstand, but it didn't hurt him; he was already dead. The head shot had canceled him instantly, as well as his motor reflexes, which was—Kelly knew—the only way Andy could save the black prostitute.

She was screaming at Andy and pummeling hard fists against his barrel chest, saying, "You could have killed me, you pig bastard! You pig! You bastard!"

Andy pushed her away, onto the bed, saying, "You're very friggin' welcome, lady. Name a kid after me."

The blonde had found her way over to a chair in the corner, where her whimpering continued, accompanied by tears as she tried to curl onto its seat in a fetal ball.

Kelly sighed and holstered his weapon. The smell of cordite hung heavily in the air. He could hear commotion in the hall, and he stepped out, holding up his shield, shouting, "Police! Stay back!" and heads popped back into rooms.

When he came back into the hotel room, Kelly found Andy, .38 still tight in his fist, kicking Viana's dead body in the side.

"You had to do it, didn't you? You son of a bitch. Scungilli prick—"

Kelly put a hand on Andy's arm.

Andy's eyes were wild. "The bastard made me shoot him, John. Shit! Now I *lost* that toupee-wearin' turd. God! Damn! Shit! I lost Giardella."

"We'll get him, partner. We will."

Andy kicked the burly corpse again, in the stomach. "I wish he could feel that."

"Well, he can't," Kelly said calmly, "and you're interfering with state's evidence, and scaring the girls, here. Shall we make some phone calls?"

FOURTEEN

It was after visitor's hours, but the doctor let him in to see her anyway. Sipowicz viewed her first through the window blinds of the single-patient room in Intensive Care, where a nurse with a clipboard was monitoring the girl and the machines keeping her alive.

She still looked pretty, or as pretty as a girl can look with tubes running up her nose and into her mouth, and wires hooked to her bandaged chest like she was a damn car getting a jump start. Her eyes were closed, but the doctor had told him she'd been drifting in and out of consciousness since the operation this afternoon.

He held her hand—gently, as it was the hand connected to her I.V.

Her eyelids fluttered open; the china-blue eyes

were delicately lovely, absurdly so in this terrible context.

"H-h-hi," she said.

"Don't try to talk."

"H-h-hard round . . . this."

She meant the tube in her mouth.

"Don't talk," he said, leaning in. "I just wanted you to know I'm here."

She nodded, barely; smiled a little, around the tube.

"Why don't you squeeze my hand, Shayna, once for yes, twice for no."

She squeezed it once—not much of a squeeze, but enough.

"You know what happened to you? That someone shot you?"

Her mouth tightened around the tube; she squeeezed once.

"Giardella had this done to you. He's not your friend. He's a very bad man. You have to accept that, Shayna. You have to know that."

She squeezed his hand.

He went on: "The man Giardella sent to do this to you is . . . you just need to know, I handled it."

"J-j-jail?"

"He was trying to hurt two other girls. I had to take more serious measures."

"An . . . Andy—"

"Don't talk. Just rest. The doctor says you're doing fine." That wasn't exactly the truth, but she did have a shot. It was possible she could pull through this. It was. It was.

He continued: "When you're better, I'm sendin' you home. I got a little money for you, and we'll call that aunt of yours, and you'll, you know, finish high school . . . then college . . . theater arts, maybe. That'll be nice. Won't that be nice?"

She smiled around the tube; squeezed his hand.

"Maybe meet a nice boy . . ."

A smile; a squeeze.

"You just rest. I'm gonna be outside . . . right outside."

She squeezed his hand twice.

"Naw, I can't stay, honey. But look . . . " He swallowed hard. "I want you to know . . . I'm there for you. I got a son, over in Jersey, but I wasn't there for him." He scratched his neck. "I'm gonna ask you something. I never had a daughter. A little girl. You think you could think of me like that? A second dad?"

Smile. Squeeze.

"And you're a second kid, for me, right? A second chance, too. I'm gonna tell you somethin', Shayna. I ain't had a drink all day, and hey, let me tell ya—I'm way overdue. But I'm here for you. Understand? I'm not gonna be some sloppy drunk you can't depend on."

Nod. Squeeze. The blue eyes were wet with tears.

Sipowicz glanced around him, to make sure nobody was watching; then he leaned in and brushed her tears away, gently, with a handkerchief, and he kissed her forehead.

He squeezed her hand again, and she squeezed back, and he gave her his cheeriest smile, and a thumb's up, and went out into the hall. He found a chair in a little waiting alcove and sat and fought the gnawing in his gut, battled the craving that coursed through him, dying for a drink but holding out against it.

About an hour later, things got very bad, and Sipowicz suddenly did something he hadn't done in a long time, not since the day he'd lost his faith, a day he'd come across a father who'd done something terrible to his baby, a day he'd gotten drunker than he'd ever been, and he'd been plenty drunk.

He prayed.

FIFTEEN

The doctor, a middle-aged bearded man with eyes that had seen too much, said to Kelly, "I can talk to him."

"No," Kelly said. "No. I'll do it."

Andy was sprawled in a chair in a waiting area down the hall from Intensive Care. His head was back, his mouth open; he might have been dead. Then he began twitching, fighting demons in his sleep.

Gently, Kelly laid a hand on his partner's shoulder and shook him awake. "Andy . . . Andy. You gotta wake up, now."

The big man bolted forward and startled the hell out of Kelly. Andy's eyes were wide and filled with fear; he was breathing hard.

"She's dead, isn't she?" he said.

Kelly swallowed. Then he nodded.

Sipowicz collapsed back into the chair; his mouth was slack, his eyes empty. "That's what I get."

Kelly pulled another chair around and sat across from him, leaned forward. "What do you mean?"

"Nothing. I was right the first time."

"What are you talkin' about?"

Andy grunted a humorless laugh. "I stopped praying, last year, after that bastard killed his . . . you remember."

Kelly nodded.

"Well, earlier this evening . . . I decide to stop drinking. I figure if she can make it, I can make it. But I figure we both could use some help. So, hey, I figure what better time to get some support, what better time to get back in communication with the man upstairs."

Kelly was shaking his head. "It doesn't work like that."

Another grunt of a laugh. "You're tellin' me. I'll tell you how it works. It works like this: people stop gettin' hurt by low-life bastards when somebody puts those low-life bastards to sleep."

"Don't do it, Andy."

"Do what, John?"

"Don't kill Giardella. Take him down. Do it right. But do it like a cop. That's what you are."

Andy shrugged it off. "Naw, I used to be a cop. I'm just another saucehead now. Just a former human who's pulling his partner in the sewer with him." Andy's mouth tightened and he thrust his arm out, pointing down the hall. "*I* got that girl killed in there. I got drunk, and spilled to that whore Lois, and she spilled to Giardella and—"

"Stop. Don't do anything tonight."

"Somebody's got to do something—"

"Not tonight. Promise me."

"I'm not promising anything."

"Promise. Promise you won't kill the son-of-a-bitch. Andy? Promise."

Andy said nothing. His mouth was tight with fury; the bags under his eyes were black, his eyes themselves shifting here to there, as if trying to escape their sockets. If he'd been breathing any harder, the hospital would have had to hook him up to a machine.

"Andy—I know about loss, 'kay? I . . . I lost my dad in a hospital like this. Some rat bastard shot him down, and prayers didn't save him, didn't help him pull through. Why? I haven't the slightest idea, but I do know one thing: you're the closest thing to a father I've had since my dad died. And I'm not up to losing you, too, over this."

"I'm nobody's father . . ."

"You're my friend. You're my partner. Don't do this. We'll find a way. We'll put Giardella's ass in fucking stir. You murder him, you're just another scumbag."

"Maybe I am."

Kelly glared at his partner, grabbed him by the arm, hard. "You owe me. I got shot because of you, right?"

"Jesus, John—"

"Did I get shot because of you?"

"Yes!"

"Do you owe me?"

"Yes. Goddamnit . . ."

"Then you promise me. Promise me you won't kill him. Something has to separate us from rabble like Giardella. Don't cross the line, Andy. Promise!"

Andy swallowed hard. Then he nodded.

"Say it."

"I promise."

Kelly sighed, patted his partner on the shoulder. "'Kay. So. You need a ride?"

Andy shrugged. "Naw. I still got the unmarked. I'll drop it off at the station house. Walk home from there."

"Good. You want company?"

"No."

"'Kay, then. We're cool?"

"Yeah."

Andy got up, twitched a smile, ran a hand over his thinning hair, and went over to the elevators. He pushed Down. Then he turned to his partner.

"See you tomorrow, John."

"Tomorrow, Andy. You know, you saved that girl's life."

Confusion creased Andy's forehead. "What?"

"That black girl up there in the Howard Johnson's. That dickhead would've wasted her."

"Yeah." A *ding*, and the doors to the elevator at left slid open. "Now she's got a full life ahead of her.

Maybe she'll become a nun and work in a leper colony or something."

"Maybe," Kelly said with a tiny smile. "Anyway—it was a hell of a shot."

"We'll see if the Rat Squad holds a similarly high opinion of my approach to police work."

And Andy stepped on the elevator, the doors closing as he nodded good night.

Kelly sat there for a while; then he said a prayer for his partner and was just rising when the doors of the elevator at right glided open and Laurie stepped out.

She looked great, and she looked terrible; she'd obviously come from home, not work, because she was in a patterned blouse and jeans, purse on a strap over her shoulder. Her face was puffy, particularly around the eyes. She'd been crying.

But mostly she looked mad.

"There you are," she said dryly.

"Jesus," he said. "God, Laurie—I know I shoulda called . . ."

He moved to meet her and she walked past him and sat back down in the waiting area. She was staring straight ahead. Already he didn't like this. He let out some air, then went over and took a seat next to her, turning to face her as her eyes bored a hole in the wall in front of her.

"I waited till seven," she said, "then I forgot about my pride and just called the station house. I was told you'd been involved in a shooting, and that you were at St. Vincent's Hospital."

"Oh, hell, Laurie, that was irresponsible of—who did that? Who did you talk to?"

"It just caused momentary confusion," she said, her smile so small it barely qualified. "It didn't take long to find out you were fine—that you weren't at St. Vincent's because you'd been hurt or anything, but that there was a gunshot victim you were checking on—"

"It was this kid, this girl Andy took under his wing," he said. "She died about fifteen minutes ago."

"I'm sorry."

"Andy just left."

"He cared about this girl?"

Kelly nodded. "Yeah. She was a fourteen-year-old runaway he was trying to help get home."

"Doesn't sound like Andy."

"Yeah, really it does. I guess . . . you know, I know him better than you."

She looked at him now; her expression was cold. "I'm sure you do."

"He just went down the elevator before you came up."

"Yeah, well I didn't run into him."

"Hmmm. Well, I'm sorry about the mix-up. I got no excuse . . ."

"I know you don't."

He gave her half a grin. "You, uh . . . want to get a pizza or something?"

"It isn't that easy, Johnny."

"Look, I'm sorry—"

"This just isn't working."

"What isn't?"

"This."

"This?"

"Us," she said.

Was this the moment he'd been fearing? He felt nervous, far more nervous than he had today when he and Andy were about to burst into that hotel room where a murderer waited.

"We been doin' okay," he tried lamely. "This weekend, didn't that turn out nice? The lodge, the fireplace . . ."

"The sex is always good, Johnny. It's just not enough."

He tried the little-boy smile. "It's a start, isn't it?"

"No, it's where it *started*. Now—now, it's just becoming a way to change the subject."

"What is the subject?"

She looked him right in the eyes. "The subject is, we just don't get along. I'm not saying it's all your fault. It's mine, too. We're just not there for each other."

"We can work on that."

"I don't think so."

He swallowed; his mouth was dry, his tongue thick. "Laurie, what are you saying?"

She shook her head in slow frustration. "I'm saying you were in a goddamn shoot-out today, a man was killed, and you didn't even call me. Then you didn't show up for supper, and you didn't call, and I sit there worried, imagining the worst, where the hell is he, what could have happened? Was there a shooting, another shooting?"

Her voice was trembling now.

"Laurie, I'm a jerk. I just got caught up in this . . ."

She was looking at the wall again. "We're just not a team, Johnny. We love each other. We're friends."

"Best friends."

She shrugged. "Maybe. Friends, at least. But not a team. Not like you and Andy. Sometimes . . . nothing."

"What? What is it?"

She was crying. "I feel like such a bitch."

He risked slipping his arm around her. "Laurie, please . . ."

"I'm jealous of that drunken asshole partner of yours," she said, fumbling in her purse for a tissue. "He's got a part of you I've never gotten close to."

He tried to kid her. "Hey, I never slept with Andy."

She looked at him again, eyes brimming with tears. "I told you, Johnny. This isn't about sex. Making love has never been a problem for us. Living together, that's the stumbling block, isn't it? You smothering me, me nagging . . . yes, damnit, nagging, because of the fear of what you do for a living, that you'll go in the 'wrong door' someday, like your father. I'm not up to it."

He sighed. Gestured gently. "We could talk to a counselor . . . a priest."

"I've talked to a lawyer."

He drew back. "A lawyer? When?"

"Last month. I didn't go through with it then. But I'm going to now."

"Go through with what?"

"Getting the separation papers drawn, Johnny."

"No, Laurie—"

"Yes. Do you want me to look for a place?"

"No! Hell, no!"

She snapped her purse shut; the little sound echoed in the hallway with an awful finality. "Then I want *you* to start looking. I have to ask you to sleep on the couch, until you find something, because I don't trust you or myself, and I want you to start looking right away. Try to be out by next weekend."

"This isn't right, Laurie. Don't do this."

"My mind's made up, Johnny."

"We'll go home, we'll talk—"

"We're not going to stay up all night talking about it. I'm staying with my friend Julie tonight. She drove me over here."

She stood.

He looked up at her and his eyes begged her to reconsider.

She softened for just a moment, touched his face. "I'm glad you're all right."

And then she turned and quickly moved to the elevator; when she pushed the Down button, the door immediately slid open and swallowed her up, and Laurie was gone.

"Detective Kelly?"

He turned. It was the doctor.

"Do you want me to notify the girl's next of kin? She gave me the name of an aunt, this afternoon."

"No," Kelly said. He stood. He drew in a breath, then let it out. "I'll do it. Goes with the job."

The doctor handed Kelly the slip of paper, and the detective trudged to the nearby pay phone.

SIXTEEN

Rain battered the roof of the unmarked car as Sipowicz sat parked across from Neglio's Coffee Shop on the corner of Mulberry and Hester. It was close to ten o'clock. He hadn't taken a drink yet, not one drink all day, and he was burning with the desire; but something else burned hotter.

He had followed Giardella and his two front bumpers—one of whom had been at the wheel of the mobster's money-green Cadillac Seville—the few blocks from Giannini's Roma Antica Restaurant, where creature-of-habit Giardella dined every Monday and Thursday night.

The wig-wearing scumbag had undoubtedly sat at the best table in Little Italy's most expensive restaurant, raising a toast to the late Salvatore Viana.

Of course, Giardella had no doubt failed to mention how he'd maneuvered Sipowicz into doing his dirty work for him—and how that must have frustrated the fat slob. Sipowicz could imagine how Giardella would like to have been able to brag that up to the other assholes who frequented the place.

But this piece of cleverness Giardella would have to keep to himself; it wouldn't do to let his associates know how readily, how gleefully, he was prepared to betray them.

Now Giardella was in Neglio's, probably paying his respects to his *capo*, Angelo Marino.

While Sipowicz sat watching through the rain-streaked window, cracked slightly to air out his cigarette smoke, he noted one of the front bumpers—the pompadour pretty boy from Minetta's—hauling out a big open cardboard box from a side door of Neglio's. Wearing no raincoat and getting his fancy suit spattered by rain, the bumper juggled the box awkwardly around as he worked a key in the trunk.

Sipowicz smiled as he watched the pretty boy, awash in the deep blue neon of the Neglio's sign, stow the box away, shut the trunk, and head quickly back into the coffee house.

You don't suppose, Sipowicz thought to himself, *by any chance, there's contraband in that box?*

Monday nights, as it got later, Giardella liked to make the rounds of the Centerfold Lounge and his other clubs and establishments of erotic entertainment; Monday was a slow night, a good night for Giardella to chat with his management and not be bothered by any citizen who might recognize one of the better-known mob celebrities in the city.

Could Giardella be dropping off somthing illegal to one of his places of business? The mobster had been known to buy liquor and other items on the black market, to circumvent tax payments and generally cut corners.

The rain was coming down pretty good now. Light traffic hurried by; the sidewalks were damn near empty. Sipowicz thought for a second. That all-night drugstore on Mott, wouldn't they have a little hardware section? He was all of a sudden in the mood for some do-it-yourself repair work.

Fifteen minutes later, the rain was driving down, and a blue-neon—bathed Sipowicz was driving a nail into the Cadillac's right rear radial. Then he hammered in another nail, and another, and it felt so good swinging that hammer, and another, and another . . . .

When the rain let up, Giardella and his pair of front bumpers got into the Cadillac, and barely a block from Neglio's, the damnedest thing happened: the car had a flat.

Sipowicz pulled over, and got out of the unmarked car. The Cadillac's driver—not the pretty boy, but the zit-faced blue-eyed bodyguard in whose lap Sipowicz had dumped the marina sauce at Minetta's the other day—got out and came around behind the car, kicked the flat tire, and opened the trunk to get at the jack.

"You got a problem?" Sipowicz asked the guy, ambling up, showing him his shield. "Anything I can help you with, from a serving-the-public stand-point?"

The zit-faced bumper immediately recognized Sipowicz and glowered at him, saying, "Somebody gave us a flat tire."

"*Gave* you a flat tire?"

The back door of the Cadillac opened and Giardella climbed out; he wore an expensive dark green suit that complimented the lighter green of the Caddy nicely. His open shirt revealed curls of chest hair where a gold chain nestled; his shiny Italian loafers splashed the puddled water in the street as he came around to kneel and examine his flat tire.

"Sipowicz," he said, looking at the nails in the radial, "this is childish even for you."

"You got some *nails* in that tire, Al?" Sipowicz asked, leaning against the rim of the trunk, keeping it from being closed. "You musta drove by a construction site or something. Or some of the nails you tack your rug on your skull with mighta fell out, that's another theory."

Giardella, fuming, came around, pushed his bumper out of the way, and faced Sipowicz. "This constant harassment, you asshole, it's gonna stop."

"It's not harassment, Alfonse. I'm just a police officer routinely surveillin' a known felon. Oh! What's this in plain sight?"

Inside the box, cartons of cigarettes were stacked, around thirty or so.

Sipowicz plucked one of the cartons out. "I don't see any tax stamps on these cartons. It's a good thing

I don't need probable cause, with the trunk standing open like this. Are you aware, Mr. Giardella, that this is illegal merchandise?"

"Hummer busts," Giardella muttered contemptuously. "That's all you're good for, you nickel stiff. . . ."

"Could I see your registration, please, and license? I need to ascertain ownership of this vehicle. In the meantime, you have the right to remain silent."

And Sipowicz slammed the fat hood against the side of the Cadillac, patted him down as he finished reading him his rights, then brought Giardella's hands behind his back and cuffed them. The hood's front bumpers looked on in helpless confusion.

Thirsty as he was, Sipowicz could wait till after he got Giardella down to Central Booking. Small as this victory was, it would be worth celebrating at Patrick's. The one thing he hadn't lost faith in was the amnesia he could find in a glass.

"This isn't over, Sipowicz," Giardella snarled as the detective dragged him toward the unmarked car.

"You're right, Alfonse," Sipowicz said with the nastiest little smile he could muster. "It's only the beginning."

ABOUT THE AUTHOR

MAX ALLAN COLLINS has earned an unprecedented seven Private Eye Writers of America Shamus nominations for his Nathan Heller historical thrillers, the most recent being *Carnal Hours*, 1994, winning twice for *True Detective*, 1983, and *Stolen Away*, 1991. The new Heller, *Blood and Thunder*, is a 1995 Dutton hardcover.

A Mystery Writers of America Edgar nominee in both fiction and non-fiction categories, Collins has been hailed as "the Renaissance man of mystery fiction." His credits include four suspense-novel series, film criticism, short fiction, songwriting, trading-card sets, graphic novels, and occasional movie tie-in novels.

He scripted the internationally syndicated comic strip DICK TRACY from 1977 to 1993, is co-creator (with artist Terry Beatty) of the comic-book feature *Ms. Tree*, and has written both the *Batman* comic book and newspaper strip. His current comics project is *Mike Danger* for Tekno-Comix (co-created with bestselling mystery writer Mickey Spillane), also in development as a major motion picture by Miramax.

In 1994, he directed, wrote and executive-produced *Mommy*, a suspense film starring Patty McCormack and Jason Miller. He is also the screenwriter of *The Expert*, a 1995 HBO World Premiere film.

Collins lives in Muscatine, Iowa, with his wife, writer Barbara Collins, and their son, Nathan.